ELVIS WEEKEND

Inspired by Real Events

Written by

KATHY ROCCO

"Do something worth remembering."

Elvis Presley

ELVIS WEEKEND

Cover design by Kathy Rocco

ISBN: 1475143591

ISBN 13: 9781475143591

Printed in the United States of America.

Dedicated to my mother,
the most beautiful woman I know.
At 90 years old this year,
you are a blessing, a joy,
and an inspiration.
God Bless You, Mom.

PROLOGUE

ᴏ3ᵹᴐ

It's Friday evening, August 14, 1987. The Phillips family is busy packing for their much anticipated weekend trip to the lake. Paul and Amy are anxious to get away for a few days leaving behind the stress of work and busy life in the city. Their two sons, Brad and Matthew, are talking non-stop about the fish they plan to catch and the blue-belly lizards that have gotten away on previous visits. They can hardly wait until tomorrow morning to begin the drive to their favorite destination.

It's also the 10th anniversary weekend of the death of Elvis Presley. Elvis Presley died on August 16, 1977.

ᴏ3ᵹᴐ

"Ambition is a dream with a V8 Engine."

Elvis Presley

There is something special about the time that the Phillips' share at their lakeside vacation home. It's unspoken, but the feeling is evident among all of them. For Paul and Amy Phillips, it's always a welcome getaway from their very full lives in the city. They relish the peaceful and picturesque lakeside town of Pleasantry nestled deep within the cool verdant forested mountains of Northern California.

Pleasantry, with its quaint shops and meandering shoreline pathways, has been host to an array of adventures over the years. Everything from spending the day boating on the beautiful lake to fishing off of their private backyard dock or picking plump wild blackberries among wide-eyed friendly deer to simply enjoying beautiful sherbet sunsets and a bright white moon serenely floating in the night sky among countless twinkling stars.

Wrapping their days and nights like a special gift, the scent of healthy green pines gently carried in off of the lake on sheets of cool breezes and light misty sprays is rejuvenating. There is no other smell like it, joyfully lingering in memory and easily recalled.

Together with friends, or just with their family of four, the Phillips have spent many memorable weekends and vacations at the lake. They especially enjoy leisurely strolling the main street of the friendly little town and investigating the variety of shops and eateries, bicycling along the sunny lakeside paths, discovering the areas abundant nature, and participating in the small town's local activities.

Pleasantry's beautiful blue lake is the small mountain town's main attraction. Known for its crystal clear water and abundant supply of fresh water fish, the lake is also home to a variety of birds and forest animals that inhabit the surrounding trees and lush green natural landscape. Sparkling mountain streams and creeks carry melted snow water and mountain spring water from higher elevations that continually feed into the beautiful lake keeping the water level stable and fresh. Run-off via small brooks and creeks, carry the lake water to lower level farms for irrigation.

The Phillips handsome nineteen foot mahogany Chris Craft, upholstered with white leather, sits ready to go at the end of their backyard dock. They often spend an entire day on the beautiful peaceful lake water skiing, swimming, floating on cushions, enjoying snacks, and a picnic lunch.

At the end of a full day of boating and sunshine, there is no more relaxing feeling than the gentle rock of the Chris Craft as it maneuvers the late afternoon current heading back to shore. A light cooling and refreshing spray sometimes drifts into the boat dousing the boys in the back seat who are covered with towels in anticipation.

Always with a healthy tan after a day on the water, the Phillip's enjoy a warm shower, a backyard barbecue, and an evening of relaxing out on their backyard deck watching the brilliant sun go down on another beautiful and perfect day at the lake.

The Phillips waterside vacation home was built in the early 1900's by Paul's great-grandfather and still has the charm of that era. A mix of mature blue spruce, flowering pears, colorful maples, and white birch trees are clustered around the property giving shade and privacy to the small white board house. The circular driveway paved with intricately placed old red brick surrounds a sparkling little lily pond. An inviting gray cement bench set on golden flagstone pavers provides a front row seat for viewing the lily ponds half dozen colorful coy that often jump up out of the water to everyone's delight.

Off of the driveway, a golden hued earthy slate stone walkway welcomes guests to the white railed wrap around porch and red front door with black weathered hardware. A small old rusted wheel barrow overflowing with ivy and bright flowers make the gray board porch cheerful and inviting. The Phillips lakeside cottage home is simply charming.

The Phillips boys, Brad and Ryan, love to fish off of their backyard dock or along the sandy shoreline of the beautiful lake. The boys keep the tradition started by their great-grandfather of logging their catches in the Phillips Family Fishing Album that rests on a small dark oak table in the living room surrounded by old framed pictures of their ancestors showing off some of their favorite catches.

Although their days usually begin early with fishing pole in hand, their other favorite all-time lake activity is catching blue-belly lizards among the rocks and tall grass. Days at the lake are full of endless fun and exploration. From the moment the boys rise in the morning until their sleepy heads rest against their pillow at night, they are happily immersed in all the wonder and discovery that the town and lake have to offer.

PROLOGUE

The lake has always been the Phillips special getaway place. Whether in cool winter rain showers or bright eye-squinting sunshine, each weekend and vacation at the lake have added to their favorite family memories.

Little did they know the mystery and intrigue that awaited them, and that *this* weekend was going to be the most special of all...for every one.

CHAPTER 1

Paul Phillips likes to get on the road early for the three hour drive to the lake. At 7:00 a.m. he is restless. Turning on one side and then the other, his thoughts wander pleasantly through the years of past lake memories and settle on the anticipated morning drive ahead of him.

Suddenly, the ring of the alarm clock jolts him. He quickly silences it with a swat and lay there for a moment collecting his thoughts. He glances to see if Amy is awake. Quietly he rises, sitting on the edge of the bed, his tan smooth back arching as he stretches and yawns in the early morning light.

The golden hardwood floors are cool on his bare feet. Hopping on one foot and then the other he looks almost boyish as he slides into khaki walking shorts, his favorite brown leather sandals, and comfy white BMW t-shirt.

"Okay everyone, rise and shine," Paul bellowed out into the hallway to wake the boys.

"Okay, dad, we're getting up," Ryan and Brad answer sleepily in unison.

"Me too," Amy yawned, turned over, and pulled the covers up close around her neck. "I'll be up in a minute."

Paul sat down on the edge of the bed near her. Playfully he lifted a corner of the bedcovers, found Amy's nice warm feet, and gently kissed her toes.

"Rise and shine, Sweetheart," he teased lovingly.

"Oh, that feels *so* good." Amy stretched and purred with pleasure.

"How about a little you-know-what before we get on the road this morning?" His smile turned to a grin. He looked playfully but longingly at her.

"How about a little of this…" Amy pulled him to her, gave him three quick kisses on the lips and one lingering kiss before she pushed him away.

"That's a start!" His grin was even wider now.

"Well, that's it for now, Buster!" Amy sat up, running fingers through her morning hair.

"Awe, you're no fun," he pouted, then quickly pulled the covers off of her, scooped her up out of bed, and cradled her in his arms. Amy shrieked with delight as Paul swung her around and around in the early morning sunlight that drifted in through their soft white panel sheers. A little dizzy they both fell back onto the bed in laughter.

"Paul, you're a crazy man." Amy laughed, and looked over at her husband with an adoring smile.

"You know how I love going to the lake. It gets me all twitter-pated!"

"Twitter-pated?" Amy raised her eyebrows. "You've really slipped over the edge this morning."

"Later on, if you're a real good girl, I'll show you my twitter." He loved teasing her.

"So, what are you going to show me if I'm a *bad* girl?" she shot back.

"Oh, baby, now you're talkin." He reached for her but she quickly slipped off the bed heading for the bathroom to get ready.

"Damn, you're quick!" Paul stood up and watched her disappear into the bathroom. As the door was about to close, Amy opened it just enough for him to see her wink and smile. Then she quickly closed the bathroom door behind her before he got any more ideas.

Paul and Amy are a good couple, fun-loving and devoted to each other.

Paul was first into the kitchen. The sweet husky aroma of his favorite grind wandered throughout the house as he brewed a fresh pot of hot coffee and packed a few snacks for the drive. When Amy entered the kitchen, he greeted her with a steamy hot cup fixed just the way she likes it, with a little cream and a teaspoon of chocolate.

"Mmm, thank you." Amy smiled and took a sip. "Would you check on the boys while I finish up here? Breakfast will be ready in two minutes."

Amy set out a box of Cheerios, a plate of sliced banana nut raisin bread she baked the day before, bowls, spoons, napkins, small glasses of orange juice, and a bowl of raspberries picked fresh from their backyard garden. The four of them quickly ate the healthy breakfast and just as quickly cleared the table. There was only one thing on their minds this morning...getting on the road to the lake.

When they finished eating Amy let the dog and cat in. She always makes sure they have plenty of food and water.

The family pets often make the trip to the lake, but not this weekend. Maxi, a very handsome black and tan dachshund, barked at Sasha, a feisty shorthaired orange tabby cat, as she ran past him tail up. Maxi always likes to ride in the car, head out the window, biting at the wind, ears flopping...but not Sasha. Sasha is much happier to stay at home and even happier when Maxi stays with her. They are a team. They both have the run of the backyard and the protection of the garage.

Amy juggled two bowls full of dry kibble, more than enough food for both of them for the weekend. Maxi and Sasha followed her through the mud room and into the garage where they each have a wicker basket bed and their favorite chew toys. They know the routine.

"Okay, you two. Let's settle down. Sit, Maxi, sit!" Maxi obediently sat at Amy's feet, his sparkling brown eyes darting from one bowl to the other. "Good boy, Maxi." Sasha continued to tease Maxi pawing at his head and ears. Maxi kept focused on the bowls of kibble. "Little Miss Sasha, leave Maxi alone." Amy set each bowl down a distance apart. She stepped back and watched them each run to their bowls. "You two behave yourselves while we're gone. No fighting." Maxi and Sasha did not appear to be listening.

The Phillips purchased their sweet dog, Maxi, from the neighborhood pet shop when she was just six weeks old.

His adorable little face and large bright eyes melted their hearts. Several years later, Sasha joined their family, when she followed the boys home from school one day. Paul never liked cats, but Sasha has turned out to be his pal. She follows him everywhere and over the years Paul has softened.

Paul Phillips is an aggressive business man who made good decisions and investments at the right time with successful start-up companies in the challenging Silicon Valley environment of Northern California. Paul is well-known and respected for his good business sense and fair work ethics within the technology and business communities of the San Francisco Bay Area. He isn't afraid to take a chance on ventures that he believes in and it has paid off handsomely for him and for his family.

At age 39, he is physically fit…a result of good family genes, eating well, bicycle riding, and daily power walks as his busy work schedule permits. Not to mention his love of good swing music which he and Amy enjoy dancing to whenever they get the chance. Paul's slightly graying thick dark hair is striking against his tan skin, enhancing his turquoise blue eyes and straight white teeth. With a passion for old cars and sporty motorcycles, he is a well-grounded, interesting, and likeable guy.

Amy is an attractive, petite, energetic woman, who regularly volunteers at the children's school, in the children's ward at the hospital, and at their neighborhood church. She wears her straight dark shoulder length hair down but she looks terrific with it pulled back into a ponytail.

She is a member of the Los Gatos Beautification Committee and an avid gardener. She daily tends to her fifty plus roses and other plants in the yard and tries to make time to enjoy her favorite corner...an area planted with colorful perennials, lavender, mint and a few tall fragrant redwoods that serve as a backdrop for her large white iron gazebo. This is Amy's special place to read, write, drink tea, and to reflect...a private area for thought, solitude, and inspiration.

On the left of the gazebo, a large three-tiered Italian fountain centers a small rose garden. Healthy strawberry groundcover with a red stepping stone path leads to the fountains edge. Clean gray cement walkways trimmed with red brick circle the lush green manicured lawn and travel around the yard to the patio and barbecue area. Amy takes pride in the yard and garden that she has been designing and planting for years. Paul is supportive helping her with supplies and planting when needed.

Paul and Amy have lived in the same modest house in Los Gatos since they were married and have no intentions of moving. They like the neighborhood of older restored homes, the local schools, and their neighbor's pets. They decided along time ago to stay put and that's what they are doing.

A white wooden picket fence surrounds the front lawn of their 1950's two-story wood frame and brick home. The inviting white wood archway and gate, built by Paul, opens to a straight red brick walkway and a step-up wide brick front porch. White columns and white gridded windows with flower boxes flank each side of the shiny white front door. Inside, golden oak hardwood floors, two large fireplaces, heavily veined smooth gray marble countertops in the open kitchen and family room, formal living and dining room separated by a shiny black grand piano, three bedrooms, three bathrooms, a den, and laundry room comprise the floor plan.

The large but cozy rooms are decorated tastefully and comfortably without clutter. Area rugs bring warmth to their mix of modern day and mid century furnishings. An open oak staircase leads upstairs to the bedrooms and two of the bathrooms on the second story. The two car garage with shop area is connected to the house by a glassed-in breezeway and mudroom that Paul and Amy added last year. Yes, the home is uniquely theirs and they are happy there.

Brad age twelve and Ryan age nine, complete the Phillips family. The boys are both good students in school, have lots of friends, and are liked by their teachers. Brad is more serious than his talkative active little brother. Despite their differences, the boys are best friends. Brad is a thin freckle-faced fair-haired boy with bright blue eyes. He likes animals and birds, and loves to play baseball, video games, and swim. Ryan is a medium built dark-haired little boy with deep brown eyes. He likes bugs, enjoys drawing, playing with his Hot Wheels cars, building with Lego's, and swimming. Together, the boy's all-time favorite sport is fishing and catching blue-belly lizards at the lake.

By 8:00 a.m. Paul is happily backing the car out of the driveway. They are on the road to their favorite destination, the little lakeside town of Pleasantry.

An hour out, the sweeping curves of lazy country roads began to lull away the stress and tension of work and school in the city. Paul and Amy look forward to this early morning travel time, chatting and listening to oldies on the car radio. Sometimes they sing along to their favorite tunes and reminisce about their early days together.

This morning nearly every radio station is playing Elvis music and featuring Elvis trivia. There are special activities, tributes, concerts, and television shows in his honor going on all over the country. Amy and Paul love Elvis music making this mornings drive especially enjoyable.

Open fields carpeted with rows of green vegetables and stalks of golden grain, and hillsides dotted with clusters of cows, sheep, and horses are a peaceful vision in the early morning sunlight. The pleasing smell of newly plowed earth, bailed hay, and dew covered wild mint gently flows in through the car vents as they travel along the narrowing country roads and closer to their destination.

Midway through the trip, Paul often stops at their favorite fruit stand. He and Amy like to purchase fresh produce for the weekend and stretch a little before continuing on. They enjoy the almonds, dried apricots, and other natural healthy snacks that the little fruit stand has to offer.

On the road again, they pass through a variety of small mountain towns. The trees become more and more lush and the anticipated smell of tall green pines and majestic redwoods surround them. Soon they will be entering Pleasantry.

Brad and Ryan always fall asleep in the back seat of the car on the way to the lake and today is no exception. As Paul slows the car to enter the main street of Pleasantry, Amy gently wakes her sons.

"Are we at the lake yet?" Brad mumbled, opening his eyes with a big yawn and stretching his arms out wide. Ryan was still curled up under his favorite blanket. “Hey, Ryan, wake up! We’re here!” Brad nudged his little brother. Soon Ryan was sitting on the edge of the seat beside Brad.

“Yes, we are here!” Amy announced with excitement, waving to shop owners just opening up for the day. Some were sweeping walkways and watering plants, while others were working in their display windows, but everyone took the time to smile and wave as the Phillips family slowly drove by.

CHAPTER II

ଔଓ

The warm August mid morning sun was shining brightly. A familiar gentle and fragrant cooling breeze welcomed them as Paul pulled his BMW into the circular drive of their lakeside home. They all jumped out of the car anxious to start their weekend.

"Come on boys. Help your old dad unload the car. Then we can have some fun!"

The boys began to move a little faster now. After a few more yawns and stretches they were ready to help carry in the weekend supplies.

Amy went ahead to open up the house. She slid her key into the front door lock and hesitated just for a moment. She knew what awaited her inside. A smile pierced her lips as she gently and slowly pushed the door open wide and entered. She stood there for a moment in the cool darkened house and breathed in the sweet musky smell of vintage. She loved that smell. Then she walked from room-to-room to see if everything was in place, and it was. She opened up all the paned windows and French doors to bring in the summer lake breeze. Then she settled in the kitchen to put away the groceries.

"I'll put the flag out, dad," Brad called to his father.

"Thanks, son," Paul called back, with approval and pride.

Brad carefully took the folded American flag down from the storeroom shelf, walked slowly with it through the kitchen, out onto the back porch, and down the steps into the backyard to the tall silver flagpole near the waters edge. The flag was special to Brad. It belonged to his grandpa Phillips who passed away when Brad was eight years old. Brad and his grandpa Phillips were close. Brad followed him around like a shadow from the time he could walk and grandpa Phillips loved it. They spent many hours together fishing and boating on the lake. Grandpa Phillips taught Brad all of his fishing tricks and told him all of his fishing stories. They were great pals and it was hard for Brad when his grandfather passed away a few years ago. Time has a way of healing the hurt and now Brad shares all of the good memories of his grandpa and fishing tips with his little brother, Ryan.

Raising the flag is a family ritual with the Phillips. The flag is put up when they arrive and taken down just before they leave. It's also a signal to their Pleasantry friends and neighbors that they are in town. Dotted around the lake a variety of flags bellow in the soft lake and mountain breezes. At night all the flags are lit up by spotlight. It is a beautiful sight and just another thing that makes the lake so special.

The Phillip's comfy lakeside home is mostly furnished with estate and garage sale finds. Amy and Paul both love collecting old things. Their charming home is nostalgic, warm, and cozy with each room decorated tastefully. Paul's great-grandfather who built the original house in the early 1900's, would be pleased to know that it has stayed in the family and continues to be enjoyed by his great-great-grandchildren.

Each generation has made improvements to keep the little house in good repair. When the house was passed on to Paul, he and Amy took out a wall between the kitchen and living room to create a feeling of openness. The old raised brick fireplace, once hidden in a corner, is now open to both rooms. In the kitchen they replaced two small windows with large bay windows across the back of the house to maximize their view of the lake. They also replaced their bedroom window and the kitchen door with French doors that open out onto the wrap around porch and deck. This was their way of contributing to what their parents and grandparents had generously left for them to enjoy with their own family and for future generations to come.

The wrap around porch, that the Phillip's added to extend their living space, is furnished with white wicker chairs and tables with colorful overstuffed cushions. A variety of flowering planters and containers create pleasant sitting areas in various locations around the porch. The Phillips have spent many hours there visiting, eating, entertaining; enjoying sunsets, birds, and fish jumping in the lake; and relaxing in the peace and tranquility of their little lakeside paradise.

The boys share a large bedroom decorated with fishing gear. A small old wooden fishing boat that belonged to their late grandpa Phillips stands on end in one corner of the room providing storage for their books and games. The blue sky and clouds ceiling that Amy painted connect down the wall to tree tops of a forest scene with shoreline of a sparkling lake.

A cozy guest bedroom and a bathroom are across the hallway. At the end of the hallway is Paul and Amy's bedroom. A large quilt covered over-stuffed bed on a beautifully hand tooled vintage walnut frame and headboard is the focal point. Every wall of their bedroom is painted a different pastel color...misty mint green, sheer baby blue, sandy tan, and soft pale yellow. The ceiling and all the trim work is white. Bedside dressers, lamps, a large antique wardrobe closet, two old comfy over stuffed chairs, a round top coffee table with magazines, and lots of framed artwork blend it all together. Decorating is another of Amy's favorite hobbies.

The sun was bright and high in the cloudless noon sky. A light cool and refreshing breeze brought in that familiar smell of lake water through the open French doors and into the kitchen. Amy was making sandwiches for lunch. Paul was in the yard cutting up some fire wood. The boys were hunting for lizards among the rocks and tall grass. Their grandpa Jim, Amy's father, had shown Ryan and Brad how to make a lizard catcher out of a long weed when they were just little boys. They have been making lizard catchers ever since and have caught many lizards of all shapes and sizes. Some get to ride home in a shoe box back to the city for sharing in school, but most get to stay at the lake.

Paul finished cutting the firewood and carried a bundle in to stack on the hearth. He stopped in the kitchen to wash his hands just as Amy finished making the tuna sandwiches for lunch.

"Let's eat out on the back porch." She knew Paul would like that.

"Okay, I'll bring the glasses and drinks out." As he passed her in the kitchen he slowly ran his hand over her tight jeans and gave her a little pat on the bottom. "Nice," he winked.

"Hey, cut it out!" she said laughingly, balancing the sandwich tray. "Can't you see that I have my hands full?"

"I had my hand full just a minute ago," he teased.

"Paul, you're asking for it!"

"Yes, I am and I want to know when I'm going to get it." He didn't miss a beat.

"Oh, my gosh! You are such a horn dog!"

"You mean hound dog, don't you?" He went right into song: "*You ain't nothin but a hound dog a rockin all the time...*"

"Watch out Mr. Hound Dog. You're going to spill those drinks if you don't quit fooling around."

"Okay, okay, Elvis has left the building...but just for the time being. He'll be back!" He lifted his upper lip, like Elvis and they both laughed. Paul was a fun guy with a great sense of humor and timing. He always made Amy laugh and she loved it.

"Boys, lunch is ready, come and wash up. The lizards will still be there waiting for you," Amy called, as she set the sandwich tray down on the large round glass topped iron patio table. The boys came running, washed their hands at the kitchen sink, and returned to the back porch for lunch.

"Did you see that banner spread across Lakeside Drive when we drove through town this morning? It was advertising a dance at the Fireman's Hall tonight. It said something about Elvis. Did you see it?" Paul lifted his upper lip like before, but no one noticed.

"I did see it but I didn't get all the information. I'll ask Janie what it's all about when she and Mark come to pick up the boys in a little while. I think we should all go. I'm sure it will be for the entire family."

"Let's take a walk into town after and we can check it out. It might be fun." Again, Paul lifted his upper lip to imitate Elvis. This time they all noticed and everyone laughed. It was always fun at the lake.

Janie and Mark Mitchell live in San Jose, a neighboring major city to Los Gatos where the Phillip's home is not far from them. They also have a vacation home at the lake. Like Amy and Paul, they have been coming to Pleasantry for years with their children, Matthew and Sara.

Matthew, a sturdy little freckle-faced boy with auburn hair is Ryan's age. Sara, a cute slim talkative girl with long strawberry blond hair and large blue eyes, is Brad's age. The families get along famously...enjoying many meals, fishing, town activities, lakeside walks, and bike rides around the lake together.

Mark Mitchell is a technology consultant for a major computer software company in Silicon Valley. He and Paul always have a lot to talk about. Mark is a tall medium built man with dark wavy hair, a broad smile, dimples, deep brown eyes, and a great contagious laugh. When Mark isn't working he tinkers with his collection of old motorcycles. His garage is neat and clean with every tool, nut, and bolt perfectly organized. He also enjoys gardening and grooming the yards of their home in Almaden Valley, a sunny upscale suburb of San Jose, California.

Janie Mitchell is a medium built bright-eyed perky strawberry blond who teaches fifth grade in a private elementary school. She is a fun-loving, hard working woman who is admired by her students and colleagues, and adored by her husband Mark, her children, and anyone that knows her. Participating in elementary school activities, including PTA Treasurer and Hospitality Hostess, and her love of cooking keep her busy. She especially likes baking and trying new recipes. Her once slim figure is a little fuller now, but she still looks good. On occasion, she makes time to pursue her other favorite past-times of reading mystery novels, gardening, and bicycle riding.

Mark and Janie have been a couple since high school. Together, they've made a very good life for themselves and for their children. It's obvious that they are soul mates.

Janie and Mark were coming to pick the boys up soon. Matthew and Sara had found a new fishing spot and they were anxious to share it with the Brad and Ryan. Just as the boys finished gathering their fishing gear and brought it out onto the front porch the Mitchells drove up in their red Jeep Wagoneer and out jumped Matthew and Sara.

"Are you ready?" Are you ready to go?" "Hello Mr. and Mrs. Phillips!" They called, running to help the boys with their fishing gear.

"Hello, kids!" said Amy and Paul in unison, as they walked out onto the front porch and down the steps to the circle drive to greet Janie and Mark.

"Well, how are you two?" We haven't seen you up here in a while," Mark said, as he and Janie stepped out of the Jeep and warmly hugged Amy and Paul.

"Paul had a huge project at work that kept him busy," Amy answered.

"It was grueling, but well worth the extra time I put in to make it go. But let's not talk about work right now. We're here for some r-and-r and to have some fun!" Paul didn't want to get into a heavy conversation about work.

Sara and Matthew helped the boys put their fishing gear into the back of the Jeep while their parents visited. Then the four of them piled into the back seat. It was a little crowded, but they didn't care. The kids were anxious and excited to get to their new fishing spot, but patiently chatted amongst themselves waiting for their parents to finish their conversation.

"Hey, what about that Elvis dance in town tonight?" Paul lifted a corner of his upper lip and they all laughed.

"It's at the Fireman's Hall tonight and there's going to be some special entertainment." Mark jumped up, landed in a crouched Elvis pose, and lifted his upper lip. Mark was a funny guy and always entertaining.

"Oh, Elvis," crooned Janie. "Knock it off, you big lug. You'll be scaring the wildlife away." She grabbed Mark by the arm and dragged him toward the car. "Come on, Big Daddy, you can strut your stuff tonight at the dance."

"Oh, yeah, we can work it out tonight. Right, Paulie?"

"Right on, Markie, tonight's the night!"

Amy and Paul laughed. Mark looked back at them with a big grin and a wink. He raised his arm out the window and gave them the peace sign as he turned his Jeep onto Lakeside Drive.

Janie and Mark are a great couple. They're funny and fun and have become very dear friends of the Phillips family over the years.

CHAPTER III

The boys will be back from fishing in a few hours. It's enough time for Paul and Amy to leisurely stroll into town and check out some of their favorite shops.

Janie told Amy the dance was celebrating the music of Elvis Presley. The men were to dress like Elvis and the women to dress like 1950's teeny boppers. Pleasantry's volunteer firefighters were sponsoring the dance. Money raised always went for a good cause. The Phillips like to support the small town's activities when they can. So, of course, they will all go to the dance tonight.

After Janie and Mark left with the kids, Paul and Amy locked up the house, and walked hand-in-hand into town only a few short blocks away.

There are no traffic signals and very few stop signs in Pleasantry. The bright sun was warm and high in the sky. It was a beautiful walk with a light scent of mint and lemon grass in the air. A welcome breeze off the lake gently rustled through the town's tall shade trees that lined every street. Neighbors along the way were out in their yards grooming, watering, and gardening. Everyone they passed waved or stopped briefly to chat. Children rode bicycles and some played barefoot on the grass. Dogs seemed to smile as they wagged a friendly tail. Cats just looked up sweetly, stretched, and continued to bask in the warm sunshine. It was a perfectly delightful day in the town of Pleasantry.

At the far end of Lakeside Drive, looking over the town like a proud mother hen over its chicks, the beautiful baroque and stately old City Hall building stood tall. A variety of interesting eateries, antique shops, and specialty shops stand side-by-side at the other end of Lakeside Drive, the main street of town. Heavily scrolled black iron light posts with large colorful hanging flower baskets look down on ornate iron benches, bicycle racks, and large overflowing pottery urns planted with ivy, mint, and miniature rose bushes all in bloom. A dozen small ironwork patio tables and chairs sit street side in front of the weathered wood, brick, and stone buildings that house the various shops.

Paul and Amy love to walk leisurely along Lakeside Drive. With the assortment of shops on one side and the beautiful lake across the street, it's a pleasant and refreshing stroll. They cherish the time they spend together here and each treasure they find.

Paul and Amy notice that all the shops have a sign in their window advertising the Elvis Dance at the Fireman's

Hall. Directly in front of The Alley Cat, their favorite thrift and antique shop, the crisp white Elvis Dance banner strung high overhead from one light post across the street to another, billows softly in the cooling lake breeze.

"We haven't been in here in a while. I wonder what new treasures they have." Amy was admiring a pretty little red impression glass plate in The Alley Cat's store front window.

"Well, if it isn't the Phillips, by gum! How the heck are you two? We haven't seen you around here in a while." Old Mr. Larkins greeted them from behind the counter, as they stepped inside. The heavy dark wood plank floors worn smooth with age creaked comfortably under their footsteps.

"We are just fine, Fred. Where's Mrs. Larkins today?" Amy was distracted by the shops vintage glassware display.

"Oh, she's gettin all dolled up for that dance tonight. Are you two and the kids goin? I'm all ready to go, myself." Fred proudly stood up so they could see his Elvis outfit.

"Yep, we're all going," answered Paul, looking at something across the room that caught his eye and heading in that direction.

"Just looking to see if you have anything we can wear tonight. I'd like to take that pretty red plate in the window home with me today, too." Amy looked up at Mr. Larkins. A huge wide smile of sheer delight appeared on her face.

Fred Larkins was certainly ready for the Elvis dance. Perched on his balding head he wore a scruffy looking black Elvis wig, tilted sideways. His tight white rhinestone studded Elvis outfit showed off his little paunchy tummy and thin frame. No one knew for sure how old he was, but it was rumored that he was close to ninety. His sparkling blue eyes looked bright against his wrinkled tan skin. He sometimes said things that were a little off color or risqué but he did it in a humorous way and no one took offense.

Just then, Mrs. Larkins came out of the back room carrying a plate of warm sugar cookies with raspberry centers and set them down next to Fred.

"Ah, my favorite supper...chicken nuggets!" Fred smacked his lips. "How'd you know I was gettin hungry?"

"Fred! Have you lost all your marbles? These are my raspberry sugar cookies! Clean those glasses of yours," Alma spoke low close to Fred's good ear hoping the Phillips didn't hear.

"Hello, Mrs. Larkins. I see you're already for the dance tonight and so is Fred." Amy's smile grew even broader as Mrs. Larkins moved out from behind the counter to show off her outfit.

Old Mrs. Larkins was adorable. Her thinning white hair was pulled back into a pony tail with a big pink polka-dot ribbon. Soft pink lipstick a little outside of her lip line and vivid blue eye shadow over her clear blue eyes made her look bright and perky. Rhinestone trimmed eyeglasses, little white poodle earrings, a white blouse with pearl buttons, black and white saddle oxfords, lace trimmed pink ankle socks, and a pink with white polka dot full skirt, and lots of petticoats that made her tiny waist look even smaller completed her outfit. She was all decked out!

Alma Larkins is a sweet and friendly eighty-five year old woman who the years have been kind to. She is saucy and funny and her mind is sharp. Occasionally, she backhands Fred lovingly on the arm whenever he says something that she thinks isn't appropriate. They are a cute old couple, married for sixty-five years. Everyone in town knows them and looks out for them.

Amy went to see what Paul was so intently looking at. She couldn't help but giggle softly as she prepared him for the vision of Alma and Fred dressed in all their Elvis glory.

"Well, my little chickadee, I'd like to see you wear this tonight!" With a twinkle in his eye, Paul held up a skimpy little black and red see through sexy teddy.

"I bet you would. No such luck, Buster. Give me that thing." She quickly grabbed it from him and put it back on the rack.

"Aw!" Paul complained teasingly, as Amy dragged him away from the rack.

"Come on. Let's get these few things so we can be back before the boys get home from fishing." Amy put her arm through Paul's and they walked to the counter.

"Help yourself to a warm cookie," Alma Larkins offered.

"Looks like chicken nuggets to me and tastes about the same." Fred knew just how to push Alma's buttons.

Alma put her hand across Fred's forehead as to feel for a fever.

"The man's sick. He's sick, I tell you. Fred, you're askin for it. Don't mess with me. I'm not in the mood for your poop today!" Alma Larkins is a feisty one.

Only a brief chat with old Mr. and Mrs. Larkins while they paid for their purchase because Paul couldn't keep a straight face. They each took a warm cookie to go and enjoyed it on the walk home.

Janie Mitchell dropped the kids off at the new fishing spot. She told Sara and Brad to set their watches. She would return to pick them up at 3:00 p.m.

The new fishing spot, not far off the road, was perfect for the four young anglers. The kids anxiously carried their fishing gear down the slight embankment to a small sandy beach at the crystal clear waters edge. It was a beautiful day for fishing, sunny with an occasional refreshing light breeze.

Sara spread out a blanket on the beach. She had a radio, potato chips, and some soda to share.

The kids each set up a folding fishing chair in front of the blanket, side-by-side, with tackle box underneath and bucket for their catch behind the chair. After hammering pole holders into the sandy beach soil they were ready to fish but not before they each put on their good luck fishing cap. They chattered constantly while setting up, but once the hooks were baited with red wiggly worms and the lines were cast into the water the chatter turned to a whisper. Now they were serious fishermen concentrating on the tip of their rod waiting for the nibble.

Sara's radio was softly playing "Jail House Rock" by Elvis Presley and then came the local radio announcer with a commercial about the Elvis dance.

"Okay, guys-n-dolls! It's time to rock-n-roll tonight at the Fireman's Hall as we celebrate the music of The King! All you Elvis fans come on out and shake it up tonight! Five dollars at the door gets you in and all the soda pop-n-popcorn you could ever want! Dance to the rock-n-roll tunes of The Royals oldies band and don't be surprised if there's an appearance by a very special guest! Don't miss out on the fun! All you guys-n-dolls, youngsters-n-oldsters, grandma-n-grandpa, too! Put on your best Elvis get-up or fifties outfit and come on down to the Fireman's Hall at 8:00 p.m. Be ready to shake it, rattle it, and roll it on out tonight!"

"You are going tonight, aren't you Brad?" Sara smiled sweetly at him.

"Yeah, who else is going?" He hadn't seen her in a while. The sun shining on her long blond hair hanging down from under her cap caught Brad's eye.

"I talked to some of the other kids in town and everyone will be there. It's going to be so much fun!" Sara was excited.

"Cool!" Brad tried not to stare at her. He concentrated on the tip of his fishing rod.

Something caught Brad's eye, glistening in the water.

"Hey, Rye...look! It looks like something shiny stuck in the sand. Will you wade out and get it? I'm just getting a nibble." Brad pointed into the shallow water just a few feet from shore.

"I'll get it," Ryan kicked of his sandals and gently tip-toed into the cool lake water.

"Can you see what it is, Rye?" Brad was still concentrating on the tip of his pole.

"It's a clam shell, an open clam shell." He held it up for his brother to see then tossed it to him.

"Dig a little, Rye. See if it's a clam bed. That would be cool. We can catch catfish or bass with clams." Ryan wanted to impress Sara, but he knew she was just as knowledgeable about fishing and bait as he was.

With both hands Ryan dug down deep into the soft sand and came up with three closed clams.

"Keep digging, Rye, and get a bucket. Wait until dad hears about this!" Brad remembered the stories his grandpa told him about using clams for bait to catch the biggest fish in the lake.

"Matthew, come help me dig and bring a bucket," Ryan called to his friend who seemed to be looking toward the nearby forest.

Together Ryan and Matthew dug up two dozen small clams then placed the half full bucket near Brad and Sara who quickly began to inspect each closed clam shell.

"C'mon. I wanna show you something. Don't say anything. Just follow me." Matthew whispered to Ryan.

"Hey, Sara, I saw a small bunny hop into those trees over there. Ryan and I are going to see if we can find it."

"Okay, but don't be gone too long." Sara took good care of her little brother.

"Follow me, Rye. Watch our poles," Matthew called back to his sister and Brad as the two boys ran toward the tall trees.

Matthew and Sara found the new fishing spot last weekend. But, Matthew didn't tell his sister what he found in the nearby trees. He wasn't really certain *what* he found, but he knew it was something special and he wanted to share it with Ryan.

Ryan and Matthew walked for a short distance through the tall trees until they came to a small clearing. On the left was an old log lying partially covered with dirt and rocks. They stepped over the log and continued on ducking beneath the low hanging branches of the tall forest trees.

"Mattie, where are we going?" Ryan had never been this deep into the forest before.

"Shh! Whisper, Rye, I think we're almost there. I hope I can find it, again." Matthew looked back to make sure that Ryan was close behind him as they made their way through and under the dense trees and bushes.

"Find it? What are we looking for?"

"You'll see. You'll see, Rye."

Before long the distant sound of soft music playing was all that could be heard above their own heart beat and an occasional twig snapping beneath their feet. Ryan continued to follow, staying close behind Matthew. Suddenly, Matthew stopped.

"What's that music? Are we there? Why are we stopping?" Ryan remembered to whisper.

"It's the wall! It's the tall stone wall! I found it again! This is *it*, Rye!" Matthew was wide-eyed with excitement.

"What is this place?" Ryan whispered, scanning the dark stone wall in front of him. "What's on the other side?" Ryan immediately began to climb a tree close to the stone wall.

"I don't know. I got scared the last time and ran back to the fishing spot."

Ryan stepped on each tree branch carefully holding on tight to the branches above him. When he reached the top of the stone wall he peeked over.

"What do you see? What do you see?" Matthew looked up at Ryan. He was beyond excited.

"Wow!" Ryan slid over onto the stone wall but continued to hold onto the tree branches to steady himself.

"Climb up, Matthew. You *have* to see this!"

Sara and Brad were having a great time fishing and listening to the radio in the bright early afternoon sunshine. Their families were long-time friends and the kids had grown up together. Lately, Brad was feeling like Sara had a crush on him. They always had fun together so it wasn't any big deal, especially since Brad really liked Sara.

Suddenly, Sara took Brad's hand and placed it on her leg below the knee and hemline of her jean Capri's. "Feel this!"

"What is it?" Brad squinted, feeling uncomfortable touching her leg.

"No more hair! My mother finally let me shave my legs!" Sara shared her special news with him.

"Well, feel this!" Brad took Sara's hand and rubbed it on his cheek and chin. "I'm shaving, too!" He tried to sound manly but really he wasn't shaving at all.

"Brad, will you dance with me tonight?" Sara smiled sweetly at him.

"Sure." He didn't know what else to say. "Let's have some chips and soda?" He quickly turned to look for the snacks that Sara brought with her.

Sara reached around onto the blanket and grabbed the chip bag just as the radio announcer's deep voice broke in.

"This is your one and only groovin radio station at the lake. Station LAKP playing the songs of The King! Whether you're bathin the baby, or takin the dog for a walk, or enjoyin the rays out on the lake...groove it and move it to the tunes of LAKP. We're playin your favorites every minute of every day and night! And, speakin of night, don't forget tonight! Come all decked out and ready to rock 'n' roll and jump 'n' jive to the live sounds of The Royals at the Fireman's Hall! It's Elvis night and it's gonna be a night to remember! See all you cool cats tonight at 8:00 p.m. wearin your finest Elvis or fifties outfits! We're gonna rock it and roll it out tonight!"

Sara and Brad were just packing up the fishing gear as Matthew and Ryan returned.

"Where have you guys been?" Sara sounded a little bossy. "You've been gone for a long time!"

"We were just looking for that bunny, but we couldn't find him. Did you catch any fish?" Matthew looked into the buckets to avoid eye contact.

"Look at this! You two missed some good fishing today!" Brad held up his bucket full of little crappie already cleaned and ready for the frying pan. Sara did the same.

"Maybe we can come back tomorrow." Ryan looked wide-eyed at Matthew for approval.

"Yeah, let's come back tomorrow!" Matthew readily agreed with Ryan.

Just then Mrs. Mitchell pulled up. The kids finished gathering their fishing gear, put it into the back of the Jeep Wagoneer, and jumped in for the ride home.

When Janie dropped the boys off after fishing, she and Amy talked about the Elvis dance that evening.

"We'll meet you inside on the right of the dance floor near the stage at 8:00 p.m. Okay?" We'll get a table for all eight of us. It should be fun. Wait until you see Mark tonight. He's been practicing his Elvis moves all afternoon." Janie rolled her eyes.

They laughed together and gave each other a hug good-bye.

"See you there!" Janie waved out the window as she drove away with Matthew and Sara.

CHAPTER IV

ଓଃ

Brad placed his bucket of fish in the kitchen sink. He knew his mother would want to wash the fish better and wrap them before they went into the freezer. Then the boys put their fishing gear away in the fishing locker that their grandpa Phillips built in the laundry room off the kitchen.

"Dad has the burgers almost cooked, so wash up good and meet us out on the back porch. You can tell us about the new fishing spot." Amy put a hand each son's shoulder. She sensed Ryan was teasing Brad about Sara. "Ryan, you stay here and wash up in the kitchen sink. Go ahead Brad, use the hall bath." She winked at Brad to let him know she understood.

Amy prepared one of their favorite lake dinners; grilled cheeseburgers on sesame seed buns, baked beans, sliced fruit, green salad, and lemonade. She set the table with a centerpiece of a half dozen small framed pictures of the boys when they were toddlers showing off their blue-belly lizards. The pictures were surrounded with pine cones, leaves, and rocks from the property. The boys loved it.

As they ate, the boys talked about the new fishing spot and the clam bed they found. But, Ryan didn't talk about the tall stone wall and what he and Matthew saw on the other side, at least not right away.

"I left he bucket of clams on the laundry room floor, but I put a rag over the top of it. Is that okay, mom?"

"It's perfect, Brad." Amy smiled with approval.

"I know a secret!" Ryan blurted out. "It's Matthews and my secret and no one can know about it." He couldn't keep it to himself any longer.

"So, what's the secret, little man?" Brad teased.

"Bradley!" his mother warned. "Go ahead Ryan, we're listening."

"Well," gulped Ryan as he began to tell his story, "Matthew and me found this big stone wall hidden behind the trees in the forest by the new fishing spot."

"How did you find it?" Brad interrupted.

"Please be quiet, son, and let your brother finish." Brad was trying his father's patience.

"Matthew found it last week and he showed it to me today," Ryan continued. "I'm not sure how he even found it, but I think he might have been chasing a bunny. We couldn't see over the top of it so we both climbed a tree that was next to the wall and we looked over."

"So, what did you see?" interrupted Brad, again. He got the be-quite-or-else look from his mother.

"There were lots of tree branches in the way, but what we could see was..." Ryan hesitated, "um, *beautiful*."

"What exactly *did* you see?" Paul was curious now and looked at Amy with concern.

"At first we thought it was the Garden of Eden because of all the plants, and flowers, and trees, and water."

"What do you mean, water?" Amy asked.

"A lake in the middle with a beach and a bridge on one side, and a dolphin water fountain." Ryan was wide-eyed with excitement.

"I don't know of any property like that in this area. Are you *sure*, Ryan? You and Matthew aren't making this up are you?" Paul glanced at Amy.

"Honest dad. We really saw it and, and, and..."

"Slow down, son. Take your time." Amy tried to comfort him.

Ryan took a long drink of his cool lemonade, a deep breath, and continued.

"We heard the music, the Elvis music, like what was on the radio today. It was coming from the big white house. We wanted to see more, so we walked on top of the stone wall until we found a tree on the other side that was close enough for us to reach and we climbed down behind the bushes." Ryan was rambling.

Amy had a hard time not interrupting her son, but she could see that this was not something the boys made up. They saw something and she wanted to know what.

"We stayed behind the bushes by the stone wall. Then we saw a big building. There was a window on the side. We stood on some logs to look in. We saw a bunch of cars covered with white sheets. One car wasn't covered up. It was a big white car with gold trim and a big shiny motorcycle was parked next to it. We could see the license plate." Then Ryan stopped, took another drink of his lemonade, and sat back in his chair.

"Ryan, could you read the license plate numbers?" Paul calmly encouraged his son to remember.

"Yes, but it wasn't numbers. It was just the letter E, a capital E.

"Just an E, are you sure?" Amy shot Paul a quick concerning glance.

"Yes, mom, it was just an E."

"Okay, then what?" Paul wasn't certain of exactly what the boys saw. But he knew the story must be true.

"We walked around the back of the garage and ran up to a window on the side of the big white house. It looked like a mansion like you see in the movies."

"Did you look in the window? What did you see?" Now, Brad was interested, too.

"We saw a lot of pictures on a wall."

"Pictures of what?" Amy wanted more information. She remembered hearing rumors years ago, about Elvis Presley living in this area, but no one ever thought the rumors were true.

"Pictures of Elvis with other people. In one picture he was wearing an Army uniform. In another picture he wore a white suit with a scarf around his neck. And, there were records in frames, gold and silver records in picture frames. Then we heard two men talking in the house and we got scared and ran back behind the garage to the stone wall and climbed back up the tree. We walked on top of the wall and then we climbed back down to the other side. We could still hear the Elvis music. Then we ran through the trees and back to the fishing spot, and that's the truth, honest." Ryan was out of breath and wide-eyed.

"Well," Paul sat back in his chair, looking at Amy, and then at his youngest son. "It certainly is an interesting story. Maybe tomorrow you can show us where the secret wall is but let's put it to rest for tonight. I don't think any of us should talk to anyone else about this. Let's keep it to ourselves right now. Okay?" He looked at Brad and then Ryan to make sure they understood what he was saying and that they both agreed to keep the secret. "We have a dance to go to and friends to meet. Let's clear the table and get the dishes done, so we can get ready for the dance and go-man-go!"

Paul lifted his upper lip like Elvis as he stood up from the table and they all laughed.

Amy laid out the boys clothing: cuffed blue jeans, white t-shirt with rolled up sleeves, white sox, and tennis shoes. After the boys showered and were dressed they sat on the floor against the sofa in the small cozy front room to watch television and wait for their parents to finish getting ready.

A movie was on and it just happened to be an Elvis movie. The boys watched for a few minutes and then they heard their mother snapping her fingers to the music.

"Wow, mom, you look cool." Brad saw her first.

"Yeah, mom, you look pretty." Ryan straightened up.

"Thank you, boys, you both look pretty cool yourselves." Amy wore a short sleeved crisp white cotton blouse, a green poodle skirt patterned with little pink and gray kittens playing with yarn balls, lots of petticoats, white socks, white tennis shoes, and her hair tied back in a ponytail. Amy twirled around once and sat down on the sofa near the boys to watch the Elvis movie.

"Oh, Elvis, you send me!" Amy squealed, as Paul entered the room. His straight hair was slicked back on the sides and pulled forward into a waterfall on his forehead. He wore cuffed blue jeans, white t-shirt, and white sox like the boys, but his jeans were slung low. Black penny loafers and a blue jean jacket with the collar turned up completed his outfit. To his families delight, Paul jumped into the middle of the living room floor and danced to the music in the Elvis movie.

Amy rocked from side-to-side and snapped her fingers to the beat as Paul did his Elvis thing for the boys. The boys fell together in laughter as they watched their father's Elvis impersonation. When the music stopped he did his Elvis pose and lifted one side of his upper lip. They all laughed until they were almost sick.

"Did you know that your mother sent a telegram to Elvis Presley and asked him to come over for dinner?" Paul told the boys, as he sunk into the big over-stuffed easy chair to catch his breath.

"Really mom, did you really do that?"

"Yes, I did. I knew your father liked Elvis Presley and I thought it would be great if he could come over for dinner as a surprise for your father. So, I invited him when he appeared at the Coliseum in Oakland. He made an announcement thanking me for the telegram during his concert which your dad and I attended. It was a very magical night. Elvis Presley was a great entertainer. That's why they call him The King."

The boys looked more closely at the Elvis movie.

"That's Elvis Presley right there, isn't it?" Ryan pointed, watching the television wide-eyed. "He was in the pictures at the big white house."

"Yes, that's him." Amy confirmed.

"Where is he now?" asked Ryan.

"He croaked along time ago." Brad put his hands around his throat, rolled his eyes back, looked to the ceiling, hung his tongue out, and fell over onto the floor.

"Bradley Hunter Phillips," Amy scolded. He knew he was in trouble when she used his full name.

"Sorry, mom, but that's what I heard." Brad quickly sat up straight.

"Elvis Presley died from taking too many pills. He lived in a place called Graceland, in a beautiful mansion with his wife and daughter. He had many people who helped him with his property and with his music. Some of his fans were so devoted to him that they followed him all over the world from concert-to-concert. It was a great loss when he passed away and the entire world seemed to mourn for him. People still take flowers and gifts to Graceland in his honor to this day. His music is known and played around the world in every country and in every language." Amy wanted to make sure that the boys knew the world-wide reported facts of Elvis Presley's death.

"Your mother and I saw him in person twice before he died. That was a very long time ago. You boys weren't even born yet. There was no other entertainer like Elvis or as popular in all of music history. That's why people still love his music today." Paul was serious.

They all sat quietly and watched the end of the Elvis movie. And then it was time to head over to the Fireman's Hall.

The high mountain sunset over the lake was spectacular. Chiffon ribbons of pink, yellow, and orange streaked the dusky sky. Paul stopped for just a moment to admire it on his way from the house to the garage. At the garage, Paul slipped his special key into the large old padlock. He firmly turned the key and the padlock snapped open. Paul removed the padlock and slowly lifted the heavy garage door to reveal his pride and joy, a 1956 Ford Galaxy 500 convertible, white, with red interior. He entered the dark musky garage and carefully pulled off the car cover that protected it.

"Okay, baby. Daddy's here." He patted the trunk of the car before he opened the door and slipped behind the steering wheel. He positioned himself in the seat, inserted the key, and turned it. The old car started right up just as he knew it would. He loved to hear its deep smooth purr. It made him feel young, again. "That's it, baby. I knew you wouldn't let me down."

Slowly, Paul backed the car out of the garage, put the top down, and picked up Amy, Brad, and Ryan from the front porch. A warm evening breeze washed over them as they entered Lakeside Drive and joined the line of other vintage cars making their way to the Fireman's Hall.

It was tradition for every car to drive down Lakeside Drive and make the rounder in front of city hall at the end of the block. Some of the locals liked to go around a few times before heading over to the Fireman's Hall at the other end of town.

Paul turned on the radio to the local D.J. playing Elvis's "All Shook Up" followed by an announcement about the Elvis dance that the entire town was on their way to enjoy.

Old cars of every make, model, and color lined Lakeside Drive and every one of them had Elvis drivers or passengers. Men and boys of all ages were dressed like Elvis. Cars honked and flashed their lights and turned their radios up to the same station. It sounded like "Blue Suede Shoes" was playing all over the world. Wives and daughters, grandmas and girlfriends sat up high on the back of convertibles waving, smiling, and laughing, as they cruised the main street of town before entering the Fireman's Hall parking lot.

A large round full moon was just beginning to show above the distant tree tops and stars were faintly appearing in the pretty night sky when the Phillips family arrived. The Mitchell's red mustang convertible was already parked in the lot. Excitement filled the air as the townspeople gathered at the Fireman's Hall entrance. People happily greeted each other laughing, chatting, and enjoying the variety of Elvis's. Babies to grandpas were dressed in Elvis outfits from cuffed jeans and t-shirts to Army uniforms and sequined high collared concert suits. They were all there ready to rock and roll!

CHAPTER V

ঙ৪ঌ

The Fireman's Hall was decorated to the hilt! The red curtained stage adorned with old 45 records was glowing with spotlights. Colored balloons gently bobbed on the ceiling. The Royal's band was playing "Don't be Cruel" by Elvis Presley. A drummer, keyboard player, guitar player, base player, and lead singer all dressed in matching black tuxedoes with white shirts and bright blue bow ties were all in harmony moving in rhythm. Backing them up were two cute trim blond singers in matching blue sequined floor length evening gowns and elbow length black satin gloves.

The Hall lights were dim, but it wasn't dark. A large round glitter ball splashed the walls and floors with swirling drops of light. Twisted streamers of red, white, and blue were tacked from every corner across the room, and across the front of the raised stage. Tables draped with black and white checkered cloths and red glass candle bowls were set up in rows from the front of the stage to the back of the Hall. Couples were out on the dance floor in the center of the room, some dancing, some talking and laughing, and some posing for their friends.

At the back of the Hall, wives and children of the volunteer firemen dressed in blue jeans and white t-shirts were giving out bags of freshly popped popcorn and soda's. A big sign that read "Rock 'n' Roll Tonight" behind the popcorn area was surrounded by old Elvis record album covers.

On the other side of the Hall was the "Blue Hawaii" photo area with a mural background painted to look like a Hawaiian beach scene. A life size cardboard stand up of a tan Elvis Presley wearing a flower lei and white bathing trunks was placed near the sign that read, "Have Your Picture Taken With Elvis". Plastic flower leis, artificial palm trees, flowering bushes, rocks for sitting, and a sandy beach completed the scenery. One of the volunteer firefighters was taking pictures.

The Phillips made their way to the first table on the right of the stage to find their friends, the Mitchells, eating popcorn and drinking soda. Mark stood up and posed for them in his white high collared tight fitting Elvis outfit at first sight of Paul.

"Do I look cool, or what?" Mark was already enjoying himself.

"Definitely and without a doubt," Paul agreed, and posed next to Mark. They always had fun together. It was obvious that they were very close, more like brothers than just friends.

"What a pair these two are. Just look at them!" Janie welcomed Amy with a hug. They couldn't help but giggle at their husbands posing. Janie looked adorable in a cute short skirted pink soda fountain waitress outfit.

"Hey, Brad, you look cool!" Sara bounced up and down in front of him in her cheerleader outfit and swished two fluffy paper pom-poms in his face.

"Let's go find the other kids. C'mon!" She grabbed Brad's hand and dragged him behind her through the crowd before he could utter a word.

Matthew sported jeans and a white t-shirt like Brad and Ryan. "C'mon, Rye, let's go get a soda and some more popcorn." Matthew always knew where there was food.

"Did you tell anyone about our secret?" He whispered to Ryan.

"Did you? Did you tell anyone?" Ryan whispered back.

"Not even and no way! It's only our special secret. No one would believe us anyway!"

"Yeah, you're probably right. C'mon, let's go get that soda and popcorn." They disappeared into the crowd.

The Royal's music was rockin good. Everyone was out on the floor dancing, laughing, and having fun. Janie and Amy sat at their table visiting while Paul and Mark were off getting more drinks and popcorn.

"So, what do you think about the boy's story?" Amy wondered if she should even ask but she assumed that Matthew had told his parents.

"What story?" Janie looked puzzled.

"You know…" Amy leaned closer to Janie so no one else would hear. "The tall stone wall in the trees and what's on the other side, the garage with the cars, the license plate, and the pictures on the wall...and E-L-V-I-S." Amy spelled it out in a whisper.

"That old story, haven't you heard that old lake story before? It's been going around for years. There's nothing to it. It's just the locals talking. It's like the old treasure boat story. That's another one. You hear about it, but it's just a tale. I'm surprised you haven't heard it before."

"So, what *is* the story," asked Amy. She was really curious now.

"Which one...Elvis or the treasure boat?"

"I'll take Elvis for now. You can fill me in on the treasure boat later."

"Well, the story goes like this... Somewhere around this area is a beautiful fortress built as a refuge and secret home of Elvis Presley. Elvis supposedly died at his Graceland mansion, but in reality, he was accidentally shot in the head while fooling around with one of his guns. Because he was injured so badly and needed so much medical care and recovery time, his family decided to fake his death. And that's just what they did. While the world was in mourning over his death, a medical team secretly transported him to a far off destination to do all that they could to help him recover from the tragic accident... and guess where they ended up? Right here in our own little lakeside town of Pleasantry."

"Oh, come on, now. I've never heard that story in all the years we've been coming here." Amy couldn't believe it. She heard rumors over the years that Elvis was living in the area but no one ever expanded on the why or the where.

"Well, my dear, the locals say it's true and that now Elvis and a caretaker only live there, but no one knows where *there* is! Over the years a number of media people have nosed around, but they have never turned up anything. I haven't heard talk of it in years." Janie concluded with a laugh, just as the guys appeared with the popcorn and sodas.

The band began to play "Love Me Tender".

"C'mon, baby, they're playing our song. You two girls have been chit-chattin long enough. It's time to dip-n-sway." Mark put his arm around Janie's waist and whisked her off onto the dance floor.

Paul and Amy joined them. While he held her close and sang softly to her she couldn't help think about Janie's story. But, what about the tall stone wall that the boys had found earlier that day and what was on the other side? When the song ended Paul twirled her around, dipped her back, and gave her a kiss on the lips. She liked it when it did that. It always made her feel special.

"Paul, you aren't going to believe what Janie told me. Listen to this." She just had to tell him. They stood out on the dance floor with the glitter ball sparkling overhead while Amy told Paul the story.

Soon, a drum roll and The Royals lead singer interrupted them with an announcement.

"Okay, all you Elvis's bring your best girls out on the dance floor for "The Stroll"! We wanna see you move it and grove it and shake it all around!"

The crowd cheered and the stroll line formed in front of the stage with all of the Elvis's on one side and their partners on the other. Mark made sure that he was next to his pal Paul in the line.

"Check out my sweet Janie doll over there," Mark whispered to Paul. "She loves to dance and I love watching her. Maybe later tonight she'll do a special dance just for me, if you know what I mean, old pal." Mark was always thinking.

"Yeah, I know exactly what you mean. Amy looks so fine tonight, just like when we were teenagers. I might have to lay some special Elvis moves on her, if you know what I mean, old pal." Paul didn't miss a beat and Mark was right there with him.

"Look at those husbands of ours. What could they be jabbering about? They're talking non-stop and still keeping up with the stroll line. Pretty good for guys who aren't really good at multi-tasking," Amy said, and they both laughed.

"Oh, come now. You really have to ask? What else do guys love to talk about besides s-e-x? I can tell just by the twinkle in Markies eyes that he's all wound up and probably ready to go at this very minute. Just look at him." They laughed, but Janie knew her husband well. She would be making love with this Elvis later that night. She only hoped he wouldn't want to wear his Elvis outfit to bed.

The stroll line was full. Everyone rocked from side-to-side to the beat of the music in perfect unison. One couple at a time, each Elvis and partner, moved from the stroll line out into the center and danced down the middle. A few bumps and grinds, spins and poses, and even one brave sole dropped down into the splits while the petticoats of their partners twirled around them.

The younger kids and teenagers formed their own separate stroll line. Amy could see Brad was across from Sara and soon they would be dancing down the center together. Ryan and Matthew were also in line mostly concentrating on keeping up with the beat. Everyone was having a great time dancing and laughing together.

"Okay, Janie doll...show me what you got!" Mark and Janie were now out in the middle and dancing their way down the center of the stroll line. "Go, girl. You know what your daddy likes." Janie danced beside Mark as he posed and did a few bumps and grinds in his best Elvis imitation through to the end of the line.

Paul and Amy were right behind them, holding hands, and dancing their dance together down the center.

"You look very appetizing tonight, my love," Paul whispered to Amy, as he held her close for just a moment. Amy smiled coyly. Her face flushed a little, but she didn't miss a beat. Right at the end, Amy surprised Paul with a high kick and a quick spin around. He loved it! And, so did all the other guys, as her petticoats twirled up high.

Back in line, Paul elbowed Mark. "Check out old Mr. and Mrs. Larkins!"

Alma and Fred Larkins were dancing their way down the center of the stroll line. Fred was no slouch when it came to dancing, probably why he was in such good shape for his age. He could really move it, keeping perfect time. Holding Alma's hand they did the traditional stroll with style and soul in every step. Everyone in line clapped and cheered for them. The Larkins even took a bow when they reached the end. It was all such great fun.

When "The Stroll" ended everyone stayed out on the dance floor and gave a big round of applause. No one wanted the music to end but it was time for The Royals to take a break.

The twenty minute break went by quickly. When the Royals returned, a long drum roll led to the announcement that everyone was waiting for.

"All you rock 'n' roll cats out there, we have a special guest entertainer for you tonight. He will be comin in soon, so you all get ready for the greatest Elvis anywhere in the world! But, first, we're gonna play some great oldies to get ya in the mood!"

"*Oh, little darling, boop, boop-she-boop...*" the band played and the back up singers harmonized perfectly. It was the first cha-cha of the night and everyone loved it.

"Hey, let's cha-cha-cha over and have our picture taken. It looks like there isn't anyone waiting right now. Shall we, Janie doll? Come on, you guys." Mark grabbed Janie's hand and led the way.

Paul and Amy followed. "Great idea, old pal." Paul checked the sleeves on his white t-shirt to make sure they were rolled up just right for the picture.

The young volunteer fireman was a good photographer. Often his pictures could be found on the front page of the small town's newspaper. First, he photographed Mark and Janie and then Paul and Amy and then he suggested a group photo of the four of them together.

"Stand over there near the palm tree and move in closer. Ladies, put your arm around your husband's backside. On the count of three slide your hand down and squeeze his buns. This gets a real good smile out of everyone every time."

"Now you're talkin!" Mark was elated.

"Oh, yeah!" Paul chimed in.

Even before the squeeze, everyone was smiling with just the thought of it.

"Ready? One, two, three...got it!" The photographer was right. The smiles came easily.

"We'll take two of those, my friend." Paul gave the photographer a twenty dollar bill toward the fundraiser. Mark did the same.

"Wouldn't it be fun to plan a family trip together to Hawaii? The kids would love it. We've been discussing it for a while, but Paul has just been so busy at work..." Amy slid her arm through Paul's and rested her head on his shoulder.

"I love that idea. I think we should definitely talk further about it, don't you, Mark?" Janie nodded.

"Can I wear my Elvis outfit? No because it will be too hot." He answered his own question. "Can I wear a grass skirt with nothing underneath it?"

"Let's not go there. Come on, hula-hula man." Janie grabbed his hand and dragged him toward the dance floor. The band just began playing "Return to Sender".

Paul and Amy followed laughing. Mark and Janie always made them laugh. That was one of the reasons they enjoyed being in their company so much. It was always fun when the Mitchells were around, that you could count on.

For the next half hour The Royals played some great old fifties, sixties, and seventies hits. The dance floor was full every time.

The Phillips and the Mitchells took a break back at their table enjoying the music and watching the townspeople dance. The kids danced to every single number, but the adults sat out to catch their breath and to chat now and then.

"I'm waiting to see the special guest. He might be good, but can he do this?" Mark was so funny. He raised one side of his lip and held it there, stood up, posed with legs spread wide, and moved his knee around with arms up and out like an eagle.

"Oh, Elvis, baby! You send me, you big hunka-hunka burnin love!" Janie laughed and stretched her arms out to him.

Mark held out his hand to her. She put her hand in his. He knelt down in front of her and kissed her hand gently. As he swept her off to the dance floor, he looked back over his shoulder and gave Paul and Amy a wink and lifted his lip, Elvis style. Mark had Paul and Amy laughing again.

Paul and Amy sat this one out smiling and chatting as they watched the style and moves of every different Elvis and partner on the dance floor. When the song ended, the stage lights went dark. There were a few screams from the crowd and then the room began to quiet. A dozen volunteer firemen lined up shoulder-to-shoulder in front of the raised stage.

Softly and seriously, with a light drum roll in the background, came the deep voiced announcement.

"Ladies and gentlemen, guys and dolls, here for your enjoyment is the greatest Elvis entertainer in the world. So, sit back and relax or get up on your feet and move it all around to the songs of the late....the great....Elvis Presley! And, here he is!"

A crowd quickly formed in front of the stage. The drum roll grew louder. The Royals began to play the high energy Elvis entrance, but the lights did not brighten. Ladies began to scream as a small spotlight appeared and lit the white boots and white flared pant legs of the entertainer that was moving to the beat and beginning to sing "Teddy Bear". Everyone in the Hall was dancing in place as they kept their eyes on the Elvis before them.

There was something about the way he moved, the way he sang. Amy and Paul could feel his presence. He finished "Teddy Bear" with a grand display and the townspeople went crazy clapping and cheering and trying to get closer to the stage.

He went on to sing "Heart Break Hotel". The spotlight grew wider exposing more of his trim body. A large diamond ring sparkled on the baby finger of his left hand. Amy and Paul tried to get closer to the stage to get a better look, but the barricade of volunteer firemen stopped them. No one could get through.

Finally, the spotlight widened fully and his whole body was in view but it did not move up onto his face. He appeared to be tan and healthy gyrating to the lyrics and melody as he sang "Jailhouse Rock".

With every song the crowd went wild. His tight fitting white jumpsuit was studded with rhinestones up the sides and along the unbuttoned plunging collar that revealed his tan chest. Long white fringe flowed from the left side of his wide low slung hip belt like spaghetti in the wind. A bright red scarf hung gracefully around his neck.

Amy grabbed Paul's arm firmly, "I think it's *him*! Listen to that voice and look at the way he moves. No one moves exactly like the *real* Elvis. This is *him*! I just know it!" Amy was past excited.

"It can't be. What about all the media coverage when Elvis died...the pictures, the funeral, his family mourning. What about all of that?" Paul tried to reason it out.

"I don't know. I just have this crazy feeling. I can't explain it. I think it's really him!"

He began to sing "I Can't Help Falling in Love With You". Amy and Paul and all of the other couples danced and held each other close, but no one took their eyes off of the stage and the man in the spotlight. Amy could see the glint of his sunglasses through the veil of darkness that shaded his face. He was electrifying. She closed her eyes just for a moment. She was certain that she was hearing and seeing the *real* Elvis Presley but history told her that this man was just an impersonator...a very, very good one. He ended the song with a perfect Elvis flair and pose then slid the red scarf from around his neck and threw it out into the crowd. Everyone screamed with delight. It was caught by old Mrs. Larkins, who was thrilled. The townspeople loved it. Everyone clapped and whistled...and then the spotlight dimmed to dark and The Royal's began to play the Elvis exit.

The crowd began to stomp and chant, "More! More! More!" But he did not return.

The Royals singer announced in a deep voice, "Elvis has left the building." The lights went on and he was gone.

Everyone in the Hall was still up on their feet clapping and cheering.

"Mom and dad, did you see that?" Ryan ran up to his parents with Matthew close behind. "That was him! That's the man in the pictures on the wall...that's Elvis!"

"Calm down, Rye." Paul spoke softly to his son. "He did sound and moved like the real Elvis but he was just a very good impersonator and that's all he was. He was an entertainer and he did a great job." Paul tried to sound convincing as they all walked off the dance floor to their table.

"Wow! Did you feel the presence in this room while he was here? What a great Elvis. I wonder where they found him." Janie said out loud what every one was thinking.

"He's probably just one of the firefighters making a little extra money on the side. But, I have to say, he was *damn* good…made me swoon!" Mark admitted. They all laughed but they knew exactly how he felt.

Amy excused herself from the table for a minute, but she didn't go to the restroom. She had been eyeing a doorway beside the stage that led to the back of the Hall. She quickly entered, ran down the hallway, and out the back door into the alley. It was dark and the lighting dim, but she could still see just enough. There it was...the white Cadillac with gold trim and E license plate that Ryan told them about. It was speeding away before her very eyes. She stood there speechless. The excitement welled up in her stomach.

"I have to tell Paul. I have to find the stone wall and see exactly what's on the other side." Amy ran back inside and quickly headed down the hallway.

"Oh, excuse me! I'm sorry. Are you okay?" asked a tall good looking fireman that she unexpectedly bumped into.

"I'm fine." Amy was a little out of breath with excitement. "By the way, where did you get that great Elvis?"

"Wasn't he the *best*?"

"Yes, he was terrific! How did you find him?" Amy tried not to sound too nosy.

"Well, a few days after we posted the Elvis Dance signs around town his promoter contacted us. He said that he represented the greatest Elvis impersonator of all time and that he was willing to donate his performance but with some restrictions: No one around or near the stage and no lighting on his face. He would only perform three or four Elvis songs and then leave. So, we took a chance that this guy would be good, and wow, was he ever! He was the best!"

The fireman told her all she needed to know.

CHAPTER VI

ଔ

After the Elvis act, people began to leave, especially those families with smaller children. The Phillips and the Mitchells stayed. They were having a great time dancing, laughing, and enjoying the music. They didn't want it to end but an hour later The Royals announced the last dance.

Paul held Amy close, as they danced slowly to one of their all time dip-n-sway favorites.

"Did I tell you that I love you today?" Paul whispered to Amy, as they danced cheek-to-cheek.

"Yes, in so many ways. I love you, too." Amy sweetly kissed his cheek.

"You know you're the only one for me and always will be." Paul found her lips and kissed her tenderly.

"Hey, you love birds, no making out on the dance floor." Mark leaned close to them as he and Janie danced nearby.

Paul and Amy just smiled. They didn't let Mark's comment interfere with their special moment.

The last few cords of the last dance, Paul swung Amy around and dipped her back for the finale. Amy loved it when they ended a slow dance with a dip. It was the perfect ending to a beautiful and memorable evening.

As they walked off the dance floor, hand-in-hand, Brad and Ryan excitedly ran up to them. They wanted to sleep over night at Matthew and Sara's so they could all get up early and go to their new fishing spot. Janie and Mark said it was fine with them.

The Phillips and the Mitchells left the Fireman's Hall together. They jumped into their vintage cars and headed for the Phillips house so the kids could change their clothes and pick up their fishing gear. They both turned into the Phillips circular drive, one behind the other, and parked by the front walkway.

"Come on in and we'll have a night cap while the kids get their things together." Paul likes making his specialty drinks for Janie and Mark.

"Sure, we have time." Janie and Mark agreed.

The boys ran to the bedroom to change then gathered their fishing gear and sleeping bags.

Janie and Mark followed Amy and Paul through the kitchen to the back porch deck. It was a beautiful night. A cool gentle breeze and the full moon's reflection dancing on the water was welcome tranquility after their exciting evening. Amy brought out her homemade cookies and sliced zucchini cranberry bread. Paul made his specialty iced coffee with an added shot of brandy. Amy put together a plate of treats for the kids, poured four glasses of milk, and set the platter down on the coffee table in the living room. She knew the kids would like that.

It looked like there were a million more stars at the lake than in the city. The night skies seemed crisper, clearer, and blanketed with so many twinkling stars that it sometimes seemed beyond belief. These were the kind of nights that made you just want to lay back and gaze. This was that kind of night. Amy lit a candle and placed it in the center of the patio table.

"Let's toast to a fantastic and fun evening together and many more of the same." Paul raised his glass.

"Here, here. To the best friends anyone could ask for," Mark added. They all raised their glass for the toast, clicked glasses all around then sealed the toast with the first sip.

For an hour the Phillips and the Mitchells talked about the fun they had at the Elvis dance.

The kids had their sleeping bags and fishing gear all ready to go by the front door. They watched television and ate their snack while waiting for their parents to finish visiting.

"Well," said Mark, with a drawl, and a weak upper lip after two cups of Paul's special coffee. "This Elvis is a little tired. Hey, mama. How about taking your teddy bear home and putting him to bed."

"Glad to hear he's tired tonight." Janie winked at Amy and they both laughed.

"I'm never too tired for you know what!"

"Go for it, big guy." Paul shot a wide grin at his friend.

"Don't you encourage him. He doesn't need any help in that area." Janie smirked at Paul. "Hand over the car keys, big boy. I'm driving." She held out her hand. Mark sheepishly handed his wife the keys. He knew it was probably a real good idea that she drive home.

Janie and Amy cleaned up the kitchen while Mark and Paul helped the boys carry their gear to the car. Mark wasn't much help in his relaxed condition.

Amy and Paul kissed their sons goodnight and stood at the edge of the porch waving.

"See you tomorrow. Have fun fishing…and don't forget to brush your teeth tonight!" Amy just had to add that last little reminder.

"Okay, mom," the boys called back in unison.

As the Mitchells red 1964 mustang convertible rounded the drive to exit, they could hear Mark call back to them, "Elvis has left the building!"

Arm-in-arm, snickering about Janie and Mark, Paul and Amy walked back into the house. They latched the windows and doors, closed out the lights, and got ready to settle down for the night.

When they retired to the bedroom, Amy turned on her vintage milk glass bedside lamp, removed the plump decorator pillows from the bed and placed them carefully on the green and white floral over-stuffed chair. She turned down the antique quilt and fluffed the full white bed pillows. Paul turned on his matching bedside table lamp and picked up the local lake newspaper and his reading glasses from the night stand. Paul and Amy enjoy reading at night before they close the lights.

Paul just finished the local section when Amy appeared. He looked up, peering over the top rim of his reading glasses, and quickly set the paper aside.

"Well! What do we have here?" He was surprised to see her posing for him in the skimpy little black and red see through sexy teddy that he found at The Alley Cat that afternoon.

"What do you think?" Amy slowly turned so he could get the full view of her naked body beneath the sheer fabric.

"I think you should move your sweet little self right over here next to me." Paul turned off his light and lifted the bedcovers for her. Amy gently slid into bed and snuggled into his waiting arms. He immediately and passionately kissed her warmly and deeply.

"I didn't think you liked this little number." Paul was referring to the black and red teddy.

"I thought it might be fun to wear tonight so I grabbed it when you weren't looking. I wanted to surprise you," Amy whispered into his ear, and slowly licked his earlobe with her warm tongue.

"You surprised me alright. You can surprise me like this, anytime." Paul held her close and kissed her cool neck passionately. "Now, how about turning off that light, baby doll," he crooned softly and romantically...and Amy did just that.

"What's that noise? It sounds like someone knocking on the front door," Amy thought, laying still in the darkness listening. She looked over at Paul. His even breaths and slight snore told her he was in a deep sleep.

"There it is again. Someone *is* knocking at the front door." This time she was certain of it.

Amy quietly got out of bed and slipped on her pale pink terrycloth robe. She pulled the thick ties tight around her slim waist as she tip-toed barefoot down the hallway to the front door.

"Just a minute," Amy called softly, through the closed door. "Who's there?" No one answered.

Feeling uneasy, she slowly unlocked the door but left the safety chain in place. Cautiously she opened the door just a few inches and peered out into the darkness.

"Hello, can I help you?" Amy said quietly to the stranger on her porch. She could see a man against the moonlight, but she couldn't see his face.

"Amy Phillips, I remember you." The man's voice was soft and deep.

"Remember me? Remember me from where? Who are you?" Amy whispered out into the darkness, as she tried to see his face through the night shadows.

"You know, Amy. You know who I am. I saw you tonight at the dance. Open the door. I have something for you." The stranger was convincing. He held out his hand to her. His voice was mesmerizing. It sounded familiar.

Amy hesitated briefly before obediently removing the safety chain. The door slowly swung open. She stood there facing him in the middle of the night with only the moonlight between them.

"You saw me at the dance? In an instant she knew who he was. She was standing before the Elvis impersonator, or was it the *real* Elvis? Her heart raced. Her palms grew moist. He began to walk toward her in the darkness. He reached for her. Amy froze. She couldn't move. His hand gently touched her cheek. She looked up into his mysterious wanting eyes. She felt the warmth of his body close to hers. She couldn't speak. She tried to scream but there was no sound, and then Amy awoke with a gasp. Her heart was pounding. It was just a dream! A crazy dream!

Amy couldn't go back to sleep. She looked over at the alarm clock. It was 5:00 a.m. She and Paul usually slept in until 8:00 a.m. or so on weekends. The dream was so real. She was still thinking about the Elvis dance, the Elvis impersonator, the E license plate, and Ryan's story. The more she thought about it, the more intrigued and restless she became.

After an hour of restlessness, Amy quietly slipped out of bed, wrapped up in her terrycloth robe, and tip-toed out to the cool morning kitchen. She liked this time of day when the lake was calm and the sun was just beginning to lighten the early morning sky. Misty lights twinkled from homes and boats around the lake and birds flew close over the water.

Amy drew water for tea. Waiting for it to brew, she sat on the comfy down pillow of her kitchen window seat and gazed out over the back porch onto the lake. Trying to put some reason to the events of the last twenty-four hours, her thoughts rested on the mystery of Ryan's story. She wondered if Elvis Presley could really be alive. She pulled her knees up under her robe and watched the sun come up at the far edge of the lake. So many thoughts were whirling in her head. The tea pot began to gently whistle. Amy turned to see Paul standing there in his t-shirt and shorts but not completely awake, yet.

"Oh, you're up. I hope I didn't wake you. I couldn't sleep."

"No, you didn't wake me." Paul stood there yawning and stretching. "I wasn't sleeping very well, myself. Kept thinking about the Elvis thing."

"Me, too," she confessed, and wondered if she should tell him about her dream.

Paul sleepily took the teapot off of the burner, poured the steamy water into the waiting cups with tea bags that Amy set out on the counter. He added just the right amount of sugar and cream for both of them and brought them to the kitchen table. Amy served a bowl of fresh strawberries, a block of cream cheese with a small spreading knife, and a few slices of her zucchini cranberry bread. The hot tea cups warmed their hands in the coolness of the morning. They sipped tea, ate, and reminisced about the dance and all the Elvis's and how much fun it was. They talked about Ryan's story, Janie's account of the Elvis story, and about what she saw behind the Fireman's Hall...the white Cadillac with the E license plate speeding away and what the fireman told her about how they got the Elvis impersonator and the restrictions of no one seeing his face. Amy even told Paul about her dream.

As a brilliant new day sun filled the early morning sky Paul and Amy continued their conversation growing more and more intrigued by the Elvis impersonator.

"Do you think we can find the stone wall that Ryan told us about?" Amy almost didn't want to utter the words but she did. She tried to subdue her excitement.

"I bet we can! We can ride our bikes over to the new fishing spot and park them in the trees so no one can see them from the road. Let's get ready to go." Paul was always game.

It was still early. Sparkling dew clung to their shoes as they walked to the garage where the bicycles were stored. Paul unlocked the padlock and pulled up the garage door. Passing his 1956 Ford Galaxy 500 convertible that he covered after the dance last night, he patted it on the fender and sang, "*It's alright baby*" in his best Elvis voice.

The two mile ride along the lake's edge to the new fishing spot was breezy. Their sweatshirt jackets were barely enough to keep them warm. The sunny morning sky and warming lake breeze kept them on the edge of comfortable. They were glad that it was still too early for the children to be there fishing.

Paul and Amy rode to the edge of the fishing spot and into the nearby trees. When they were well out of sight, they parked their bikes behind some bushes.

"It's cool here out of the sun and under the trees." Amy folded her arms and shivered a little.

"Yes, it is. C'mon, let's see if we can find the log that Ryan told us about." Paul put his arm around Amy with a warming little squeeze and gave her a kiss on the forehead.

CHAPTER VII

There wasn't a designated walking path in the forest, but a slightly worn area through the ferns looked like someone had walked there before. Paul followed closely behind Amy. The trees were tall and the brush was thick filling their senses with the smell of fresh pine, redwood, and mint. Although the sun was shining brightly on the lake, the dense tree branches covered them with damp shade.

They walked deep into the forest hoping they were going the right way toward the stone wall.

"Paul, there it is...the log! We found it!"

They stepped over the log just like Ryan told them and continued on. The trees and bushes grew more abundant and their branches lower to the ground.

Paul and Amy were crouching now, moving branches aside as they made their way. It was quiet in the forest. They walked slowly, carefully looking all around for some sign of the tall stone wall. Only the faint crackle of leaves and pine needles and an occasional small twig snapping under their feet could be heard above their own breaths.

"How did the boys ever find the stone wall?" Paul whispered as he held his aching lower back.

"Remember? Mathew was looking for a bunny. They easily went under all of these branches, not to mention youth." Amy continued on in front of Paul crouching down lower as the branches commanded.

"I hope we find something soon. My back is *killing* me." Paul complained.

Suddenly, Amy stopped in front of him.

"We *found* it! This is *it*! Look!" Amy excitedly reached back for Paul and pulled him up beside her.

The tall stone wall was dark and cold and almost completely hidden by thick bushes and tree branches.

"It's *really* tall, must be at least eight feet. Look, we can stand up over there." Paul took Amy's hand as they moved to the only open spot they could see.

They stood shoulder-to-shoulder with their backs against the wall, looking for a tree they could climb. They definitely were going to see what was on the other side.

"Follow me," whispered Paul.

They inched along close to the wall until they found a sturdy tree that looked like it could take them to the top.

"This one will do." Paul folded his hands to cup Amy's foot. "Step here and I'll give you a boost then I'll follow."

"I hope I can do this." Amy gripped Paul's shoulder for balance and stepped up into the tree. She placed her feet one after the other branch by branch close to the trunk climbing steadily until she reached the top of the tall stone wall.

"Can you see anything?" whispered Paul, climbing up the tree behind her.

"Not yet…too many branches in the way."

Amy stepped away from the tree onto the top of the solid stone wall.

"Paul, I'm standing on top of the wall. We can walk along it and hold onto the branches until we find a place or tree on the other side to climb down." Amy kept her voice low. Paul was now standing on the wall beside her.

"Are we crazy, or what? Look at us, standing on the top of this wall out in the middle of the woods. What if we fall? We could seriously get hurt. We could *die* out here. Who would find us?" Amy was getting nervous.

"Elvis would find us, baby," crooned Paul softly, in an Elvis voice.

"Paul, you nut! You better watch where you're going!" Amy was anxious to find a place where they could safely climb down.

Carefully and slowly, they walked along the top of the stone wall peering through the branches. The trees on the other side began to thin allowing them little glimpses of the property. They could hear water moving, birds singing, and soft music playing. Amy was in awe of what little she could already hear and see.

"Look! Up ahead." Paul pointed the way. "I think that might be a place to climb down."

Once on the other side of the stone wall Paul and Amy crouched behind the tall dense bushes. Slowly they inched along the wall looking for an opening that will allow them to enter the verdant grounds.

Peering between the bushes reveals a sparkling white mansion shaded beneath the sprawling branches of the old majestic trees that surround it. With its green tiled roof, it is very well hidden among and under the natural foliage. The mansion is definitely out of place for the little town of Pleasantry with its large paned windows and stately white columns.

As the bushes began to thin, Paul and Amy see what Ryan was talking about. Now, they understand why he thought this breathtaking beautiful place was the Garden of Eden.

A small clear blue lake edged in stone glistened in the morning sunlight and was the focal point of the expansive yard. Lush green manicured lawn surrounded the small lake and covered the yard like a velvet blanket. Tables with green umbrellas, chairs, and benches were strategically placed among the trees creating intimate sitting areas around the little lake and impeccably landscaped grounds. Urns of dripping greenery and colorful flowers softened and sweetened the area.

On one end of the lake an emerald island of tropical foliage with palm trees, rock waterfall, Koi pond, and sandy beach was as beautiful as any Hawaiian picture post card. Off to one side a noble bronze fountain of jumping dolphins spewed a rainbow of water into a steamy hot tub creating a subtle mist in the coolness of the morning air. A wooden walking bridge provided a graceful pathway gently arching from one side of the island to the lakes edge. Golden flagstone walkways led from the bridge around the yard to a magnificent slate stone patio and handsome shiny black marble cooking island with a huge polished silver barbecue. Smooth white columns supported a green tile canopy roof that shaded the entire area including the patio furnishings and a large cobblestone fireplace with conversation pit. From the patio overhang several low hung ceiling fans were slowly moving the morning air. Low growing ferns, a variety of bronze garden statues, and perfectly tended colorful shade plants completed the setting.

Right of the mansion, mounds and valleys of expansive green turf surrounded several miniature blue water ponds of a small private golf course. Two shiny red golf carts with white surrey tops were parked under shade trees nearby. A jogging path bordered the golf course leading to a white railed horse corral on the other side. Two beautiful wide-eyed golden palominos were basking in the morning sun with fresh hay at their hoofs. Clear sparkling water ran into their white porcelain trough from a large brass pump. The white French windowed open barn and tack area featured a shaded patio and picnic lawn adjacent to the corral. It was a stunning sight. Secluded and so well hidden.

Tiny song birds perched in bushes and trees could be heard over the soothing sound of the property's water features. Their sweet chirping melodies seemed to harmonize with the faint music...the Elvis music that the boys told them about. Butterflies happily floated among the flowers. Every leaf and flower on every plant, bush, and tree appeared flawless.

Amy and Paul stood frozen holding hands tightly at what they had found. Speechless, they took it all in. There was so much to look at and it was all perfectly beautiful, like no other property they had ever seen before. It was peaceful and inviting. It was paradise.

"Do you smell that?" Amy closed her eyes and drew in a deep breath. "Mint, pine, rosemary, roses, and all of the flowers combined." She opened her eyes to make certain she wasn't dreaming again.

Paul nudged her, "Look over there to the left beyond the lake and island. That looks like the garage Ryan told us about. C'mon, let's go see."

Amy held Paul's hand firmly as they tiptoed toward the large white stucco garage with green tiled roof.

"There's the pile of wood and there's the window." Paul was anxious. Together Paul and Amy peered in. It was just like Ryan described. White car covers protected a half dozen old cars, a variety of motorcycles were up on stands, and the large white Cadillac trimmed in gold with E license plate was there, too. The crisp white walls of the garage held a collection of shiny black framed pictures depicting a variety of vintage cars and motorcycles. The black and white checkerboard floor was sleek and clean. Leather jackets, caps, and gloves were hung neatly along the side wall. It was a huge garage with automatic roll up doors and large overhead light fixtures. In one corner was a round shiny red metal table with six chairs, a colorful old juke box, and an old fashion big red Coca-Cola machine. The immense garage was spotless and looked like a showroom.

"Wow! Will you look at this! What a toy shop!" Paul was delighted. "What I wouldn't give for a garage like this! Can I have one? Please, pretty mama?"

"Paul, you're a crazy man, but I love you." Amy gave him little peck on the cheek.

Paul couldn't take his eyes off of the cars. "If Mark could see this he'd think he died and went to heaven."

"Paul, come on now, enough drooling. I see the big window that Ryan told us about." Amy was looking past the garage toward the mansion. She tugged on his arm to get his attention.

Holding hands and staying low, they quickly moved from the back of the garage to the side of the mansion. Cautiously they peeked over the sash of the large window. There were gold records in frames, awards, trophies, and pictures of Elvis Presley covering every wall. The room was large with a floor-to-ceiling white stone fireplace. A beautiful shiny black piano rested on deep piled red carpet. Black leather couches and black slate topped iron tables completed the stunning décor. It was handsome, masculine, and definitely Elvis-looking.

"My Lord, look at this! If Elvis doesn't live here, who does?" Amy whispered in awe.

"I don't know but I'm beginning to feel a little uneasy about being here. I think we should go back."

"Oh, *really*..." The voice from behind startled them. Amy and Paul both jumped and quickly turned around to see who was speaking. He quietly walked up behind them and they didn't even hear him.

"What are you two doing here? Don't you know this is private property? How did you get in here anyway and what do you want?" The man peering at them through dark sun glasses was definitely serious.

He wore light khaki pants and a white linen short sleeved shirt with sleeves rolled up revealing his large tan muscles. A wide brimmed woven straw hat, finely made, shaded his dark wire rimmed sun glasses. He was clean shaven with full lips and bright white teeth. He was not smiling. In one hand he held a walkie-talkie. His other hand rested on a polished black 45 holstered in leather on his side.

"Uh, wait a minute, wait a minute! We don't mean any harm. We were just curious, that's all." Paul was almost stuttering, as he eyed the man's pistol.

"We just happened to find this place by accident." Amy crossed her fingers behind her as protection from the lie.

"No one find's this place by accident. I suggest you both come with me right now and don't say another word." The man glared at them.

"Really, mister, we don't want to interfere. We'll just tip-toe back out of here and no one will ever know we've been here." Paul tried to sound convincing.

"It's too late for that now. Do as I say and there won't be any trouble." The man quickly unsnapped the leather guard on his holster.

"Are you threatening us?" Amy nervously eyed the man's hand resting on his revolver.

"Take it as you like, miss, but you both better damned well move away from that window right now and come with me." The man meant business.

Quickly, Paul and Amy moved away from the window as he commanded.

"This way right now...and no stopping." The man gestured toward the side of the house.

Paul and Amy didn't utter another word. They didn't dare.

As they walked, Paul tapped Amy on the arm and subtly motioned for her to look to the left past the garage. Surrounded by a screen of tall dense trees, a shiny black and silver helicopter was tied down in the middle of a large clearing. Veiled high overhead a green net shade camouflaged it. They had seen this helicopter fly over the lake before, but never knew where it came from.

CHAPTER VIII

ଓଃ

The man escorted Paul and Amy to a side entrance. Two cement urns planted with small topiary trees and bright flowers flanked each side of the large door. The man stopped, entered a code into a keypad on the wall, and pushed open the heavy black door that led into the mansion.

"Follow me and stay close. We don't have many visitors here." The man was stern.

"Did you say *we*? You don't live here all by yourself, do you?" Amy tried to keep the excitement in her voice down.

The man stopped abruptly, turned, and glared at her. Amy immediately stopped talking.

He led them down a wide white hallway with tall black doors. Stopping at one of the doors, he opened it, and gestured for them to enter. It was the room they saw through the window and it was even more impressive now that they were actually inside.

"Please, take a seat. You must do as I ask. Don't leave this room and don't touch anything. I'll be back in a minute. Are we clear?"

Paul and Amy just nodded. The stately house was quiet and almost eerie feeling.

"What have we gotten ourselves into?" Paul was feeling like a kid who got caught with his hand in the cookie jar. They both sat down sinking into the comfortable over-stuffed black leather sofa.

"Look at this room. It's impeccably decorated. This leather furniture alone must have cost a fortune." Their eyes wandered taking in every detail.

"Let's see what happens when old smiley returns." Paul was trying to make light of the situation. They laughed quietly together but only briefly.

In a few minutes the man returned. To Paul and Amy's surprise, he carefully juggled a large silver tray with water glasses, a pitcher of raspberry lemonade, a small ice bucket with silver tongs, black napkins, and a plate of chocolate chip cookies. It was obvious that he knew how to serve. He set the heavy tray down on the slate top round coffee table. Then he took a seat across from them, and removed his hat revealing a head of thick silver hair. His large strong hands were smooth and his fingernails were clean and manicured. Although he was not a young man, he appeared to be very physically fit.

"Please, help yourself." He sunk back into the chair across from them with a steady look and arms folded across his chest.

Paul added ice to each glass, reached for the pitcher, and poured. Amy took one chocolate chip cookie for each of them and gently placed each one on a napkin. She did not look up at the man. No one said anything. It was uncomfortably quiet as they sipped the cool refreshing beverage.

"So," he began, breaking the silence, "I think we should introduce ourselves. My name is Cody...and yours?" The name suited him. He leaned forward in the chair, elbows on his knees, hands clasped in front of him. He looked at both of them and waited.

"I'm Paul Phillips and this is my wife, Amy. We have a small vacation home in town. Our family has been coming up here for many years." Paul rambled, not knowing exactly how much information he should give.

"Yes, we know," Cody responded, coolly.

"You know?" Amy sat up straighter and looked at Cody with questioning eyes.

"Yes, we know. We know about everyone in the town of Pleasantry. They just don't know about *us* and that's the way it has to stay. I've told you two way too much already and you've seen too much. Now, we need to decide what to do about it." Cody stood up and walked in front of them toward the window. Their eyes followed him.

"You're going to have to tell me how you found us?" Cody turned to face them. Amy noticed that he occasionally glanced past them toward a large framed mirror on the wall.

"Who else lives here with you?" Amy heard herself blurt out the words. "I'm sure you've heard the stories around town...since you seem to know everything," she said it kind of sarcastically but didn't mean it that way. She wanted to take the words back but it was too late.

Cody glared at her, but she continued. "They say that Elvis Presley is still alive and..."

"Now, wait just a darn minute, missy!" Cody quickly bristled, interrupting her. "We know the stories. They've been told around town for years. People can think what they want. That's their right. And, people can live how and where they want. That's also their right. Don't you agree?" He waited for their affirmation.

"Yes, of course we agree." Paul didn't know what else to say.

"But, you're avoiding the question." Amy added, looking at Cody and then at the mirror. "Who else lives here with you?" She hated to press him but she just had to.

"Now, look here you two, we need to talk and then you need to leave the same way you came in. So, let's get some things straight. You're going to have to answer *my* questions and then we'll see about answering yours." He looked intently at Amy and then at Paul as he stood like a giant, arms folded, before them.

"Now, how did you get onto the grounds this morning?"

Paul was nervous. "Well, our son and his friend accidentally found the stone wall when they were looking for a bunny they saw run into the trees. They were curious as little boys are, so they climbed the wall."

"Oh, now it makes sense. Those two young ones yesterday belong to you." Cody shook his head with understanding. Slowly pacing before them, he momentarily looked up to the ceiling as if everything was clear to him now.

"Only one belongs to us. The other is our friends little boy." Amy joined in the conversation.

"So, they told you what they saw and how to get here and you had to see for yourselves. Is that it?" Cody turned to peer at both of them.

"That's pretty much it. We rode our bicycles around the lake, parked them in the trees where no one would see them. Then we walked through the brush and under the trees until we found the stone wall. It wasn't easy. We climbed the wall and dropped down onto the other side and the rest is history." Paul was feeling more confident now.

"This is such a beautiful place. Our son thought it was the Garden of Eden," Amy broke in, trying to lighten the mood.

The conversation began to flow much easier and Cody seemed to be softening a little. Amy could almost see his brief smile of pride at her last comment, but only for an instant, and then it faded.

"So, who did you say lives here?" Amy was still fishing.

Cody continued to pace.

"You must understand that we are very private people. We can't have the outside world on our doorstep. I live here with my good friend who was injured in a terrible accident along time ago. He doesn't go out in public or mingle with other people because the accident left him with some facial and head disfigurement. He chooses to live a life of solitude. I live here with him and do what I can to help him take care of this place...and that's all you need to know." Cody concluded firmly. He stopped pacing to face them, standing sturdy and strong, like a wise old oak tree.

But, Amy had more questions. "Don't either of you ever *leave* this place? Of course, who would want to...it's so beautiful and peaceful here. It's an oasis. How do you get food and what about medical care if you get sick?" Amy was sitting on the edge of her seat now firing one question after another.

"We only leave if we absolutely have to. We have ways of obtaining food and I have had extensive medical training. We really don't *need* anything else." Cody looked seriously at both of them.

"You both realize how important it is that no one knows about us. We ask that you not tell anyone of what you have seen here. We trust you. You seem like good, honest, decent people...in fact, we know that you are. So, before you leave, we need to have your word that you will not tell anyone about your visit here today. If you do, there could be some repercussion that would not be very pleasant." Cody was firm.

"*Repercussion*, what does that mean? What *kind* of repercussion?" Amy was now worried that they did indeed get themselves into something that could jeopardize the safety of their family.

"You won't need to worry about it if you do as I say. Do not tell anyone about this place. Not how you found it and not what you have seen. It *has* to stay a secret kept between the two of you. As long as you keep the secret, there's nothing to worry about." Cody meant business but he didn't want to scare Paul and Amy too badly, only a little.

"We appreciate what you have shared. You can rest assured that your secret is safe with us." Paul took hold of Amy's hand, patted it in affirmation, and continued. "We can see how important it is to you. We will respect your wishes, but can I ask a favor of you before we leave?"

Amy just looked at Paul. She had no idea of what he was about to say.

"If it wouldn't be too much of an imposition, I would love to see your collection of old cars?"

Cody was surprised by the question.

"You'll have to excuse me for a moment." He glanced toward the mirror. "My friend and I will need to discus this. I'll be right back. Please, do not leave this room." It wasn't a warning. It was an order.

"What on earth are you *thinking*? Can I see your collection of old cars? I can't believe you said that!" Amy stood up to stretch a little then sat back down. "I want to know about you know who?" Amy whispered.

"Why are you whispering?"

Amy got close to him and whispered in his ear, "Because *he's* watching us from behind that mirror on the wall. Don't turn around." She continued quickly, holding his face in her hands so he wouldn't turn to look.

"What are you saying? What makes you think that?"

"Didn't you notice that Cody was glancing at the mirror as he chatted with us? I think *he's* in the next room watching us through the mirror. And I think Cody is with him right now. We can't leave here until we find out *who* Cody's friend is."

"Oh, I see…because it might be..." Paul lifted one side of his upper lip and they both fell back in the deep leather couch in laughter.

Just then Cody returned.

"Glad to see you two are enjoying yourselves. We don't have many visitors around here. It's been rather nice to entertain you." A smile pierced his lips. He picked up his hat and turned to face them. "About the cars...I'm sorry but we don't think it would be appropriate. Whatever you have seen here today is more than anyone has been allowed to see... *ever*. We really need to keep our personal lives confidential. I'm sure you understand." Cody stood firm waiting for Paul and Amy to stand so he could escort them out.

"Uh, before we leave, may I use your bathroom?" Amy asked shyly.

"Of course, it's just across the hall." Cody opened the door for her that led out into the wide hallway and watched until she closed the bathroom door behind her.

The tall black wooden door was heavy. For a moment she just stood there and surveyed the room. Golden oak planks covered the spacious floor. A huge skylight centered overhead brought in sunlight and illuminated the black gold veined marble counter top and shiny black dual sinks. Thick gold bath towels and hand towels hung neatly over long brass rods. Red fabric shades topped brass wall lamps hung on each side of the enormous gold baroque framed vanity mirror. Shiny brass faucets were elegant against the black marble counter. The colorful walls were stunning, covered in old Elvis movie posters applied with over-lapping edges to look like wallpaper. A large clear glass shower trimmed in gold was set against the opposite wall adjoining a dressing area with a mirrored closet door and a thick cushioned sitting bench. A large oil painting of a shiny red Harley-Davidson motorcycle hung over the handsome red leather bench seat.

Amy was curious. She stood in front of the mirrored closet door and began to open it slowly when a knock on the door startled her. "Are you alright in there?" It was Cody's voice.

"Oh, yes, I'll be right out," Amy answered lightly. Her heart was pounding. Without thinking she opened the closet door wide. She was looking for something, but she didn't know what. Suddenly there it was. A dozen collarless white wrap around robes with wide open sleeves and black fabric tie belts were monogrammed with the initial E. She knew immediately that they were garments worn for marshal arts. For just a moment she stared into the closet. Then she heard Paul's voice in the hallway. Quietly, she closed the closet door and stepped out into the hallway where Paul and Cody were waiting.

"Okay, I'm ready to go." Amy slipped her hand into Paul's and squeezed it tightly. He knew she had been snooping.

Cody led them down the hallway and out onto the bright beautiful grounds. He reminded them again about their promise.

"It has been a pleasure to meet both of you. We wish you and your family much good health and prosperity in all that you do in life." Cody shook each of their hands and bowed slightly to Amy, lifting his hat in a gesture of respect.

"Thank you," Amy said sincerely. "If you or your friend ever need anything, please feel free to call upon us. I think you know how to find us, right?"

Cody just smiled. "It's time that you two leave now, the same way you came in. I have work to do. Go on, now." He spoke nicely but with insistence.

Paul led the way down the side of the garage, past the little lake, and into the bushes and trees. Amy turned around to see Cody still watching them. She waved one last time.

Cody waved back. He did not take his eyes off of them until they were out of sight.

CHAPTER IX

Once on the forest side of the stone wall, Paul and Amy crouched down slowly making their way out from under the low tree branches. After standing up straight and stretching their backs they continued through the woods.

"Okay, miss snoopy, what did you find in that bathroom? I know you found something of interest. Spill it, sweetheart."

Amy told him about the white collarless robes and the monogram E on each one.

"Elvis was really into the martial arts thing. Remember how he incorporated some of the moves into his performances?"

"Oh, you mean like this?" Paul struck a wide legged crouched karate pose. Then he lifted one side of his upper lip, Elvis style.

"You nut!" Amy gave Paul a loving slap on the arm. "Knock it off! Seriously! I *know* he was there. I know he was watching us through that mirror." Amy was rambling with excitement. "And, isn't Cody an interesting man. I can understand why he's so protective, or should I say *they* are so protective of their home and property. If word ever got out about this place and you-know-who...I hate to think of what would happen to our beautiful peaceful lakeside town. It would be crawling with the media and people would flock here just like they do at Graceland. It would be a mess!"

"I think you're right, sweetie." Paul stopped walking and pulled Amy close to him for just a few seconds. "Let's find our bikes and head back home. I'm getting hungry and not just for food, if you know what I mean." Paul raised his eye-brows and gave Amy his boyish grin.

"I can't believe you're thinking about you-know-what at a time like *this*!" Amy took hold of his hand and began to drag him through the forest.

"I'm always thinking about it, you know that, just thought I would toss out the line to see if you would bite."

"Knock it off or I'll bite something!"

"Oh, would you, really? That would be great!" A huge smile of pure delight covered his face and he reached for her.

"Paul! I'm not even going to answer that one. Let's go! We really need to get out of here." She wiggled free as he attempted to pull her close to him.

At the log, they turned toward the lake and soon found their bikes hidden in the bushes where they left them earlier that morning. Paul and Amy walked their bikes out of the cool woods and into the bright warm sunlight near the new fishing spot. The heat of the sun felt good against their skin.

"Mom! Dad!" Brad and Ryan called, in unison. "What are you doing here? Did you ride your bikes over to fish with us?" Ryan was delighted at the thought.

"Well. It was such a beautiful morning we just decided to take a ride around the lake before lunch and see if our favorite boys were catching anything," explained Paul.

"Look, Mr. and Mrs. Phillips." Sara held up her bucket containing a dozen small crappie.

"She's out fishing all of us today." Brad took the heavy bucket from Sara and put it back behind her chair.

"Oh, I see." Amy gave Brad a wink of approval. Paul and Amy smiled. They both noticed how attentive Brad was being toward Sara.

"It's just luck," smiled Sara sitting down on her fishing chair next to Brads. Sara whispered something to him.

"Oh, yeah, all of us kids have been invited to a movie tonight at the Fireman's Hall. They have a lot of left over sodas and popcorn from the dance last night. So, they're asking all the kids if they wanna come back tonight for a free movie."

"It's gonna be an Elvis movie! Can we go? Can we?" Ryan chimed in.

"I think you probably can. It sounds like fun." Paul liked seeing his sons enjoying the lake and the town just as he did as a kid growing up. Amy nodded with approval.

"After fishing, ask Mrs. Mitchell to bring you both home so you can shower and get cleaned up. We're planning to barbecue and eat dinner out on the back porch tonight. What time does the movie start?"

"I think it's at 7:00 o'clock, but I'll check with my mom." Sara answered, keeping her eyes on the tip of her fishing rod. She was a serious fisherman and often out fished all of the boys.

"Sara, ask your parents if they want to barbecue with us tonight. Tell your mother I'll talk to her when she brings the boys home after fishing today. Okay?"

"Okay, Mrs. Phillips."

Sara was a responsible girl. Responsible and organized like her mother, two qualities that Amy liked.

Ryan was busy concentrating on a nibble he was getting. "I got him! I got him *good*!" He reeled in the little crappie that was flipping at the end of his line.

"He's a keeper!" Brad held up the bucket for his little brother to drop in his catch.

"Nice one, Rye." Paul called back to his son. "You kids have fun. See you alligators later."

Paul and Amy walked their bicycles up the slight embankment and out onto the lakeside path.

The bicycle ride home in the hot afternoon sun was draining. A warm familiar lake breeze swept over them as Paul and Amy followed the lakeside path past the Fireman's Hall and their favorite shops and eateries. Residents on walks, children and dogs playing near the waters edge, and shop owners smiled and waved.

Old Mrs. Larkins was sitting on one of the ornate benches out in front of The Alley Cat. When she saw Paul and Amy she stood up and waved the red silk Elvis scarf that she had draped around her neck. Paul and Amy smiled and waved back.

"I'll bet she hasn't taken that scarf off for a minute. She probably even slept in it last night." Paul laughed.

"I think she's cute. But, you're probably right about the scarf."

"Maybe she and Fred had a good time with it last night," Paul teased.

"Paul! Where is your mind? Don't even go there!" Although Amy thought he could be right about that, too.

After parking their bikes in the garage, Paul and Amy walked around the back side of the house, up onto the back deck, and fell into their thick cushioned lounge chairs. Looking out over the lake, they both slid off their shoes and socks and wiggled their toes in the gentle lake breeze.

"I'm a little tired after the ride, the climb, and the visit, if you know what I mean." Amy looked over at Paul. He already had his eyes closed. "Are you asleep? I thought you were hungry!"

"I am hungry, just resting my eyes and my body a little, just resting up for later on tonight, in case I get lucky." Paul opened one eye to see the expression on Amy's face. He loved to tease her that way.

"You could be dead and still be thinking about the same thing. What am I going to do with you?"

I'll tell you what you can do with me, in fact I'll show you." Paul pretended to unzip his shorts.

"I think I'm going to have to put salt peter in your sandwich!"

They both laughed. Amy went inside to make lunch leaving Paul out on the porch to rest.

After ravishing tuna and tomato sandwiches and a bowl of fresh strawberries from the produce stand, talk turned to the morning's activities.

"Look over there." Paul pointed toward a forested area at the left side of the lake where a section of the trees were particularly dense and green. "I think that could be the area where they live."

"They who?" the voice startled them. It was Janie bringing the boys back from fishing. "We knocked on the front door but you two didn't answer, so we knew you would be out on the back deck. The kids had a record fishing day."

The boys rounded the side of the house with their buckets and fishing gear. After showing off their catch, Sara and Matthew helped the boys carry their gear in and put it away. All of the kids were real good about helping each other. They were close friends and it showed.

"So, Janie, what's your old man doing today?" Paul smiled at the thought of his friend, Mark.

"Don't tell him I told you, but he had a little headache this morning after last nights fun, so he spent the morning relaxing. I made him some rye toast, coffee, and a large glass of tomato juice. Fixed him right up! Now, he's good to go! He's been listening to the radio all morning. It's all Elvis music and he's lovin it." Janie laughed.

"Yeah, too bad we lost Elvis when he was in his prime. I'm sure he'd still be rockin out today if he were alive." Paul glanced at Amy but she didn't respond. She didn't want to think too much about their discovery…especially not now.

Janie looked at her wrist watch.

"I better get the kids. Sara, Matthew, let's go." Janie called into the house for her children. "We need to go home and clean up. We're coming back for a barbecue tonight before the movie. Your dad's waiting for us."

Sara and Matthew ran down the back steps.

"Bye Mr. and Mrs. Phillips," they called in unison on their way out.

"Bye, kids, we'll see you in a while," called Amy.

"Hey, Janie, tell your old man that after the kids leave we'll blend up some margaritas and watch the moon come up over the mountains, maybe even do a little night fishing off the dock."

Paul loved to sit on the wooden dock and dangle his feet in the cool lake water. It was his special place to relax, breathe in the fresh air, and relieve the stress of his busy life and work in the city. He and Mark have been known to sit there for hours, pole in one hand, and cold beer in the other. Sometimes they catch a fish or two and sometimes not.

"Oh, he'll like that." Janie headed for the front of the house to catch up with her children who were waiting for her in the car.

"Maybe we can even get him to do a little Elvis thing for us tonight. What do you think?" Paul smiled with the thought of it.

"Oh, you mean Mr. Entertainment? I'm sure it can be arranged! See ya in a few!" Janie rounded the side of the house waving good-bye over her shoulder.

CHAPTER X

଼

It's a beautiful still summer evening. The lake is smooth as glass with only an occasional circle of ripples from a fish jumping out of the water. Paul and Mark sit lakeside near the backyard dock, each enjoying an ice cold beer while tending the hotdogs and hamburgers on the barbecue.

Amy and Janie boiled corn-on-the-cob, and cut up fresh fruit for a salad. The kids set the patio table with a centerpiece of twigs, rocks, and leaves, and made strawberry lemonade.

It's a perfect night for eating outdoors and enjoying the colorful early evening sky.

The two families always enjoy each others company. Conversation and laughter come easily whenever they're together.

Everyone seemed especially hungry this night. Even the kids had seconds. After dinner they all helped clear the table. Then the kids embarked on a little lizard hunting and the adults retreated back to the patio table with a bottle of Irish Cream for a short after dinner drink.

"Well, boys, you two really know how to flip those dogs and burgers. They were delicious, as usual." Janie held up her small shot glass to toast them.

Amy held up her shot glass next to Janie's to join the toast.

"Thank you, ladies. You are too kind and we really do appreciate it. In fact, later on we'll even show you how much. Isn't that right friend?" Mark glanced at Paul with a huge wide grin and gave Janie a wink.

"Mark, shush. The kids will hear you. I think we will just let that comment go, right Amy?" Janie looked out into the yard at the kids exploring and hunting among the lakeside rocks and tall grass for lizards.

"Exactly," Amy concurred.

"Look! I got one! Look! He's a blue-belly!" Ryan held up his long grass lizard catcher with a cute little lizard dangling on the end of it.

"Are you keeping him for sharing or are you letting him go?" called Amy.

"I think I'll just watch him for a while and then let him go back to his friends." The other kids gathered around Ryan for a closer look.

After the kids finished their lizard hunt and washed up, Mark and Paul drove them to the Fireman's Hall for the movie. When Mark and Paul returned, Amy and Janie were sitting on the back porch visiting. A large frosty pitcher of blended margaritas, a big bowl of tortilla chips and fresh salsa were waiting for them.

"Oh, boy, am I ready for this? I'll be happy to do the honors." Mark grabbed the glistening pitcher and poured the slushy drinks.

"Here's to good friends." Mark held up his glass to toast Paul and Amy. Janie joined him.

"Here's to many more adventures and fun times together." Paul held up his glass to toast the Mitchells. Amy joined him.

The conversation was light and fun. A little talk of work in Silicon Valley, the kids and school, gardening, cars, vacation plans, and finally the Elvis Dance at the Fireman's Hall last night. It was fun reminiscing. There were even a few lip wiggles in the conversation and some Elvis impressions. They were enjoying themselves as the sun was setting over the lake and the sky was growing dim.

"So, Janie, tell us the treasure boat story. We haven't heard that one before." Amy was curious.

"It's just another old story that's been going around here for years. They say that in the late 1800's, some members of a successful mining party passed through here on their way to the San Francisco Bay area with all of their belongings, including thousands of dollars in gold coins. They were an affluent family wanting to relocate and to start a new life. Along the way, they felt like they were being followed, so they decided to hide their fortune in gold before continuing on. They planned to return for it once they reached their destination and were settled. But between here and San Francisco they were all killed. So, they say, a fortune in gold coins are still buried here somewhere around the lake but no one knows where."

"That's a good one. I've read a lot about the Bay Area settlers but never heard *that* story before." Paul wasn't sure if he believed it or not.

"We've been talking about getting a metal detector, maybe now's the time. I think it would be fun to go treasure hunting." Amy thought it would be a great family activity.

"Hello, Mr. and Mrs. Phillips... Is this the Phillip's residence?" The stranger's deep voice filled the evening air and startled all of them.

"Who's there?" Paul stood up to see. Amy joined him at the deck rail. A tall dark stranger appeared from around the side of the house, entered the back yard, and walked up to the steps of the deck.

"Mr. and Mrs. Phillips, I'm pleased to meet you. I have something for you." He held out a large gold colored box with a white gift card on top. He handed the pretty box to Amy with a slight bow.

"What is it? Who sent such a beautiful package?"

"Let's just say, it's from an admirer. Now that I've delivered it, I will be on my way. It has been a pleasure." He bowed formally to all of them and backed up to leave. In thick silence, all eyes followed the stranger as he rounded the corner of the house and disappeared into the darkness. As quickly as he had appeared, he was gone.

"Who in the world was that? I've never seen him around here before." Janie was first to comment.

"Neither have I, but I sure would like to have that tuxedo he was wearing. Did you get a look at it, Paul?" Mark was impressed.

"Yes, I did. It was very cool looking, wasn't it?" Paul felt uneasy.

"Amy, aren't you going to open it?" Janie loved surprises.

"No, not right now." Amy felt uncomfortable and looked to Paul for help.

"Yeah, it's probably just some advertising gimmick. Amy, why don't you just take that box into the house and we'll open it later. Don't want to bore our good friends. I could use a refill." Paul spoke quickly, trying to change the conversation and reached for the pitcher of margaritas, topping off everyone's glass.

Amy quickly took the gold box inside and placed it out of sight on a shelf in the laundry room. She stopped for just a minute to take a deep composing breath before heading back outside to face her friends questions.

"So, what's going on here? A strange guy in a cool tuxedo comes into your yard with a big gold box, says it's from an admirer, and you two aren't the least bit curious?" Mark looked intently at Paul and Amy waiting for a response, but none came. They didn't know what to say.

"Look, you two, we don't mean to pry but Mark is right. Something is going on. We can see that. Are you two okay? Are you in some kind of trouble? Is there something we can do to help? What is it?" Janie ended her barrage of questions looking seriously at Paul and then at Amy. She could see how edgy they had become.

"Come on you guys, you're making way too much out of this. There's nothing wrong and there's nothing going on, right, Amy?" Paul tried to sound convincing.

"Right, we are just fine." Amy said weakly, not making eye contact, as she crossed her fingers behind her. She hated not telling them. In fact, she *wanted* to tell them. She wanted to tell them *everything* and she knew Paul did, too. But, they were afraid. They had made a promise and they wanted to *keep* that promise.

"It seems pretty fishy to me. We can tell that *something* is going on. Of course, we are curious and concerned, as well. You both know how important you are to us. If you ever want to share anything with us, you know we will listen and will keep it to ourselves. You know that you can trust us. We will always be here for you. You can tell us anything. We just want to be sure that you are both okay." Mark took hold of Janie's hand and kissed it.

Paul and Amy looked past their friends out onto the glistening night lake. For a moment there was awkward silence between the four friends.

And then they heard it... the sweeping whirling sound of a helicopter overhead. They all looked up to see the helicopter circle once and blink it's lights before quickly heading out over the lake and disappearing behind the distant tree tops. Wide-eyed, Paul and Amy looked at each other and then at their friends.

"Okay, that's it! What the hell is going on? What was that all about? Are you guys secret agents or something?" Mark's pulse began to quicken with the thought of it.

"My Lord, what are you two involved in? You have to tell us!" Janie was insistent.

"That helicopter was signaling to you, wasn't it," interrupted Mark, excitedly. "I bet you even carry guns that you hide on your body and have watches that hold explosive devices and..."

"Now, wait just a minute!" Paul jumped in before Mark could say another word. "You are way off base. Stop and think for a minute. You know us. We wouldn't be involved in anything like that. We have kids. We have responsibilities and they don't include carrying an Uzi on our hip."

"Everyone, just sit back and relax." Amy reached behind the kitchen door to turn on the flag pole light. Then she took three candles out from the patio hutch, lit them, and placed them on the table. She needed a minute and a diversion to calm her racing thoughts. "Paul, I think we should tell them." Amy looked deeply at Paul and grabbed his hand for support.

"I think you're right. We should tell our good friends."

"Tell us. Tell us what?" Janie and Mark both spoke in unison.

"Something *is* going on, but it's not what you think. As we tell you what has happened and what we have discovered, please try to keep an open mind. When we finish, we hope you will understand. But before we start, we want to make sure that you *both* are going to promise *not* to tell anyone what we talk about here tonight. This is most important." Paul waited for their affirmation.

"You're serious, aren't you? Okay, my friend, we promise. Don't we, sweetie pie?" Mark put his arm around Janie and pulled her close. Janie affirmed with a nod.

Paul squeezed Amy's hand for assurance and then they began. They told Mark and Janie all about the tall stone wall in the forest and what was on the other side, about the Elvis dance and the Elvis impersonator, and about the helicopter and their suspicions about the stranger who delivered the box. They told them about Cody and his gun. They told them everything, including their promise to Cody not to reveal what they had seen. And, about the possible repercussion that Cody alluded to, if they ever did tell anyone.

The words flowed out easily as they shared the details of their discovery with their friends. It felt good to tell someone, even though they promised not to. They felt a sense of relief and a sense of betrayal to their promise at the same time. But, they knew their secret would be safe with Mark and Janie. They just never expected their reaction.

"Oh, come now. You don't *really* expect us to believe that old story is true. That Elvis Presley is still alive and that he's hiding out here in our little town of Pleasantry. That's a good one!" Janie and Mark both laughed.

"You guys are good…really, really good. Janie, I think we should be going. It's obvious that our good friends don't really want to share what's going on with them. It's time for us to leave." Mark downed the last of his margarita and stood to stretch.

They all stood looking at each other, their faces lit only by the glow of the candles. A light breeze off of the lake seemed to suddenly wash over them. Amy rubbed her arms for warmth and then slipped her hand into Paul's, holding it tight.

"I'm sorry you don't believe us. What we told you is true...all of it. We told you because you are our good friends. We've shared so much together over the years. We wouldn't ever deceive you or kid about something like this." Amy was hurt and disappointed.

Amy and Paul didn't know what to do next. They shared their secret but their good friends didn't believe them. They felt empty.

"Wait, I have an idea! I'll be right back." Amy disappeared into the house and in a moment returned holding the gold box. She set it down on the patio table. They all stood around the box like moths to a flame. No one spoke. Amy took a deep breath, lifted the white envelope from under the black satin ribbon, and handed it to Paul. Paul slowly opened the envelope and removed the note card tucked inside.

"Oh, my God," Janie broke the silence. "It's true. It's really true. Look at the monogram...it's an E!"

"Not so fast. I'm not convinced, yet. Let's see the rest of it." Mark leaned closer to get a better look.

Hand written in bold cursive strokes, Paul read the message. *"We hope you will enjoy this small token of our gratitude."* There was no signature.

Amy pulled one end of the black satin ribbon that held the box lid in place. The ribbon gently fell from around the box. Amy lifted the lid. Black tissue paper held together with a gold seal protected the gift. Amy removed the gold seal and slowly pulled back the tissue.

"Oh, hurry up! This is way too exciting. What's in the box?" Janie was pushing.

Amy lifted out a heavy flat square object wrapped in shiny red paper. Taped to the top was a crisp white card with the name "Paul" written simply.

"This is for you." Amy handed the gift to him. Without hesitation Paul tore open the red paper to reveal a book, *Collectible Cars.*

"I can't believe this!" Paul was in awe. "I asked to see the car collection but they denied my request. This is the greatest! Check this out, Mark!"

"Oh, my Gosh, what's this?" Amy found another package in the bottom of the box with her name on it. She quickly removed the black cording and lifted the lid of the shiny gold box. A bright red silk scarf slithered out onto the table.

It was just like the one the Elvis impersonator threw to old Mrs. Larkins at the dance.

Amy picked up the scarf and held it out to Janie. "Now do you believe us?"

"I'm speechless. I just can't believe it! Who would have thought?"

"We know exactly how you feel. We had a difficult time accepting it ourselves. But, we can't change the facts or what has taken place over the last twenty-four hours." Amy was feeling much better now about sharing their secret.

Paul and Mark were busy drooling through the car book, page by page.

"I sure would love to have been with you today to see those cars." Old cars were almost like an aphrodisiac to Mark. They really got his blood moving.

"It wasn't only the cars. It was the entire garage, a garage to die for. It was every man's dream garage." Paul looked intently at Amy. She instinctively knew exactly what was on his mind.

"Oh, no, Paul...am I thinking what you're thinking? We *can't*, we can't go back there. We promised!" She knew her attempt was weak. She wanted to go back as much as he did.

"Oh, yeah," Mark was up on his feet rubbing his hands together like a kid in a candy shop. "Let's roll, old Buddy."

"I don't know. It's a little spooky, but if everyone's going I guess you can count me in, too." Janie was still admiring the red silk scarf.

"I feel funny about going back there. Plus it's almost dark and the kids might be ready to come home soon." Amy was always the practical one. She wasn't pushing it, but the thought of it excited her and frightened her all at the same time. She was ready to climb the stone wall again even though she felt uneasy about it.

"Amy, sweetheart, I think it will be just fine." Paul tried to be encouraging. "We'll stop by the Fireman's Hall, check on the kids, and drive over to the fishing spot. We'll take flashlights. Look, it's a full moon tonight. It's a perfect time to go. Okay, baby doll? Your daddy-o wants to climb the stone wall tonight, one last time. Okay, baby?" Paul crooned in an Elvis voice as he dropped down on one knee in front of her, looked up dreamily, and lifted his upper lip, Elvis style.

It was exactly what they needed to break the tension, a good laugh.

CHAPTER XI

ঔ

Amy and Janie cleared the patio table and closed up the back of the house while Paul and Mark drove to the Fireman's Hall to check on the kids. The movie was half over but the Firemen had planned an ice cream social for the kids afterwards and, of course, they all wanted to stay.

Amy grabbed some flashlights and four sweatshirts from the hall closet. She knew it would be cool under the trees even though it was a beautiful warm summer night. Amy and Janie sat out on the front porch chatting while they waited for their husbands to return.

"I can't believe we're doing this." Janie was a little nervous about the whole thing.

"I know what you mean. But, wait until you see this place. You won't believe it. It is a *paradise*, like nothing you could ever imagine. And the smell," Amy closed her eyes and breathed in deeply. "The smell is simply rejuvenating. You'll see."

Just then, Paul's white BMW rounded the circle drive. Windows were down and Elvis music was softly playing on the radio. It seemed appropriate…as a send off for their pending adventure.

"Are you two chicks available to go for a ride tonight?" Mark hung out the window with a big grin.

"Are you boys planning to behave yourselves? If yes, we'll think about it. If no, we are definitely interested." Janie teased.

"Oh, baby…my kind of woman!" Mark quickly got out of the car and opened the back door for them. Amy slid in behind Paul. As Janie leaned over to enter she felt Marks hand slide across her bottom with a little pat and a final squeeze. Janie squealed to Mark's delight.

Paul winked at Amy. They both knew what was going on.

"Let's go! The night isn't getting any younger!"

A huge spectacular moon, bright and rising, followed them around the lake to the fishing spot. Paul parked the car off the road near a leafy thicket of blackberry bushes. It wasn't fully dark yet but the stars were beginning to show.

"Here, put on these sweatshirts. It's cool under the trees. Besides, you never know what bugs might come out at night." Amy was always the practical one.

"Oh, great…don't tell me there are bugs! What kind of bugs?" Mark hated bugs. Even small spiders made him squirm.

"Not to worry, Markie. Mama will be right beside you. I won't let any little ole bugs even take a nibble." Janie made light of it but she really knew his fear.

"You promise to stay real close, mama? *You* could nibble on me of you want to and I won't even object." Mark pulled her next to him, whispered real low into her ear, and licked her lobe.

"What are you two doing over there?" Amy was wise to Mark's antics. "I hope you two are behaving yourselves."

"Okay, kids, time's a wastin, let's go." Paul handed out the flashlights. "Stay close and don't say anything. Whisper only if you have to. Is everyone ready?" He knew he didn't need to ask but he just wanted to be sure.

The evening brought a cooling dampness that blanketed the forest floor. As it grew darker, the chirp of crickets magnified. The smell of pine and nature all around them seemed wild in the night. They stayed close together. No one spoke. Paul and Amy led the way with their flashlights scanning the forest like search beacons in the night.

"We're here." Paul's flashlight focused on the log. "Okay, now comes the hard part. On the other side of this log we'll have to bend down and stay low under the branches. It's a little rough on the back but we don't have much further to go. Are you game?"

"Are you kidding? I can already hear those cars calling to me, Mark...over here...we're waiting for you. We're definitely going all the way, right baby?" Mark took Janie's hand and squeezed it.

"I'm with you all the way, teddy bear," Janie teased. She knew what he liked and she liked giving it to him. She could see his smile of approval in the dim forest light.

"Okay, let's go. There's no turning back once we get to the stone wall, agreed?" Paul just wanted to check one last time before continuing on. Everyone agreed.

Paul and Amy could tell from the little moans and groans behind them that Mark and Janie were feeling the tightness in their lower back and legs from having to crouch down low under the tree branches. They were glad it didn't take too long to reach the tall stone wall.

"Okay, we're here," Paul whispered back to Amy, Janie, and Mark as they came up close behind him. "Keep your flashlights down low and stand as close as you can to the wall. You'll be able to stand up straight, now."

"Oh, my aching back," Mark whispered, arching and stretching to try and ease the tightness. "I haven't been down this low since the last time I tried to look up Janie's skirt!" The four friends quickly covered their mouths to muffle the unexpected laughter. Mark just couldn't help himself. He always had something funny to say.

"Shh!" Paul was able to compose himself first. "Okay, everybody just relax. We're going to start the climb. Leave your flashlights here near this tree. We'll pick them up on our way out. We won't need them once we reach the top of the wall." Paul could see that the large bright moon overhead would provide all the light they needed.

Paul and Amy knew exactly what to do. They knew what tree to climb, how far to walk along the top of the wall, what tree was sturdy enough for climbing down, and where the opening in the bushes was to enter the grounds.

One-by-one, like soldiers on a mission, they each climbed the tree to the top of the stone wall. Holding on to branches to steady themselves, they carefully inched their way to the one sturdy tree that could take them down to the other side.

Just as Paul thought, the bright summer moon perfectly illuminated the grounds and small pristine lake. The mansion's interior lamps provided the rest of the light they needed to get a good view of the house and yard.

Once down, they all stood quietly in the darkness with backs pressed against the cool stone wall.

"Well, what do you think? Isn't this paradise?" Amy whispered into the night air.

Soft filtered moonlight through the tree branches and down onto the flowers, pathways, plants, and bushes made the property look like it belonged in a fairytale. It was a stunning sight and just as beautiful at night as it was by day.

"I can't believe it! I'm speechless. I can't believe you found this place and that we are actually here. Somebody pinch me." Janie suddenly squealed. Mark pinched her behind and it scared her.

"Shh! What are you doing! If they hear us we will be in a whole lot of trouble," Paul whispered, quickly and sternly.

"Sorry old friend. I just couldn't pass up an invitation like that, especially coming from the love of my life. You understand." Mark was trying to be funny but Paul wasn't having it.

"No more fooling around now. Mark, keep your hands to yourself until we get out of here. Agreed?"

"Okay, agreed. I really am sorry, old friend," Mark said sheepishly. He knew Paul wasn't happy with him.

"I think we should all take a minute to breathe in the beauty of this paradise. Let's close our eyes, take a deep breath, and store it in memory for all eternity." Amy loved the combination of the natural scents of the property... calming scents that seemed to soothed her.

They all stood perfectly still, held hands, closed their eyes, and breathed it all in. It was almost too good to be true and deeply spiritual, like being one with God and with nature. It was an awesome unforgettable experience that the four close friends shared that night.

"Okay, now." Paul snapped them all into the moment. "Let's venture out. Stay low and close together. I'll motion to you with hand gestures to move on." Slowly they followed Paul along the stone wall behind the bushes.

Soon Paul stopped and signaled to them. One-by-one they tiptoed away from the stone wall scurrying out onto the grounds like wide-eyed forest squirrels. A soft gentle breeze filled the air with a new scent...the sweet husky fragrance of star jasmine in bloom at the base of the bronze dolphin water fountain. It unexpectedly surrounded them and seemed to almost stop them in their tracks.

Paul pointed to the back of the huge garage. Mark raised his eyebrows and grabbed Janie's hand to hurry her along. At the back of the garage the four friends lined up at the window and peered in. The soft overhead garage lights provided a clear view of the cars and motorcycles inside, all neatly in a row.

"This is it, old friend. Feast your eyes on *these* toys, but no drooling. Okay?" Paul knew that Mark was going to be elated. Old cars and motorcycles were his passion.

All of the cars were covered, except for the shiny white Cadillac with E license plate, but Mark could tell by their size and shape, exactly what they were.

"Look at this, will you? What a collection!" Mark rambled off the list..."A 1966 Ford Mustang, a 1957

Chevy, a 1960 Lincoln Continental, a 1940 Ford, a 1959 Cadillac, and a 1964 Pontiac GTO! Oh, baby, look at those motorcycles…a 1955 Harley, a 1949 Harley, a 1960 Harley, a 1964 Honda, and a 1929 Indian! Look at the paint on those bikes. They are so cool! Look at the floor, the juke box, the tables, and look at the gear! I think I died and went to heaven." Mark finally stopped rambling, breathing like he had just run around the block.

"You aren't goin to cry are you?" Paul teased, knowing exactly how Mark felt. It was an awesome garage...every guys dream. "Mark, pry your fingers away from that window ledge. We've got to get going. It's getting late and we have one more stop to make before heading back."

Mark took a deep breath and sighed. "Thanks, man, for this perfect night. I will never forget this."

Janie rubbed her husbands back then took his hand to draw him away from the window.

"Follow me and stay low." Paul led the way to the side of the mansion and knelt down below the ledge of the large window. "Hug the wall," he whispered, and pulled Amy close beside him. Paul knew that Amy was anxious for Janie to see the house.

"Stay down and I'll take a peek." Amy slowly stood just enough to peer over the window ledge through the slightly open drapes and into the house. Her pulse raced with excitement. The interior lighting made the red, black, and gold decor look even more impressive. The television was on. She could faintly hear it through the thick glass but she didn't see anyone in the room. "Janie, the coast is clear." Janie rose slowly and stood beside Amy at the window.

"Oh, my God," Janie clutched her hands to her chest. "I didn't think it would be so stunning. The records, the pictures, the piano, the furnishings, it's all so, so Elvis! Mark, you have to see this!"

Mark joined the girls at the window ledge. "Oh, wow! This is so cool. What a pad! I guess you girls will be wanting to redecorate back home after seeing this. Hey, Janie, how about raising our house in San Jose and building a ten car garage underneath it...you know...for the toys!"

"Now there's an idea worth investigating." Paul stood next to Mark now and chimed in to help out.

"Don't get your hopes up, boys. I don't think it's in the budget this year. Sorry..."

"Shh!" Paul quickly interrupted Janie. "Quiet! From where I'm standing I can see someone sitting on the couch just on the other side of the curtain, probably watching TV or a movie."

Suddenly and without warning a man's white shirted arm stretched across the window and rested on the sofa back right in front of their faces. For a moment time stood still, as their eyes focused on the man's large diamond pinky ring. It took their breaths away and scared the living daylights out of all of them.

"Run!" Paul whispered loudly. He was already away from the mansion heading toward the back of the garage. He held out his hand to Amy. "Come on, darlin, we *have* to get out of here!"

Hearts pounding in fear and excitement the four friends quickly scrambled to the back of the garage to take refuge.

"Oh, my God, it was *him*! It was *Elvis*! You were right, Amy! He *is* alive!"

It felt funny to actually hear the words from her friend, but Amy knew she was right. "We can't talk about it right now. We just have to get out of here. Paul, you take the lead. Hurry...let's go!" Amy almost felt sick. She just wanted to get home.

The four friends quickly found their way back to the stone wall, climbed up, balanced along the top, and climbed down onto the other side. Mark was the last one down.

"Okay, stop for a minute, we made it. Let's just stop and calm down now." Paul found the flashlights on the forest floor near the tree and handed them out. "So, how's that for a night out on the town with the Phillips?"

"Wow, what a rush! I don't think we'll ever be able to top this one. This is the kind of night you tell your grandchildren and great-grandchildren about, right, Janie?"

"Someday you can tell them. And when you do, they'll say, there goes grandpa again with that same old story he always tells about Elvis. He's a little senile you know. But Markie, we'll know that it's true and that's all that matters. The question is..., is Elvis *really* alive or not?" Janie said what was on everyone's mind.

"It was definitely *him*, the Elvis Impersonator from the dance last night. He wore the same diamond pinky ring, the same one that Elvis always wore." Amy was certain.

"We can't tell anyone. We have to keep it a secret. We have to all promise right now to keep it a secret." Paul was serious and they knew he was right.

That night in the dark dense forest, the four friends held hands binding their promise to keep the secret. Then they began the dreaded back-breaking trek under the low tree branches and headed back to the car.

CHAPTER XII

On the drive home, the Phillips and the Mitchells decided not to say anything to the kids about their Elvis adventure. They thought it would be best for right now to keep it all to themselves, maybe even for decades. They couldn't explain it and didn't even want to try, although everything they had heard over the years...all of the rumors and the stories...now seemed to clearly add up. Elvis Presley, the King of Rock n' Roll, was alive and well living in Pleasantry, and they were the only ones that knew about it!

Paul and Mark dropped Amy and Janie off at the house and then went to pick up the kids at the Fireman's Hall. Their timing was perfect. The ice cream social was just ending and the kids were on their way outside.

"Look at this, will you? I must say, your boy's got class. Maybe one day we really will be family." Mark was thrilled to see Sara and Brad holding hands.

"Ah, young love. You remember how it was don't you, Mark?"

"Oh, yeah, those were the best years of our lives. Aren't we lucky to have ended up with the best of the best?"

"You know it," Paul readily agreed, and held up his hand to high-five Mark.

Mark quickly responded with a slap. "You really are a good friend. I can't believe what we did tonight."

"You aren't getting weepy on me, are ya big fella?" Paul tried to lighten the mood.

"Hey, kids, over here! Did you kids have a good time?" Mark called out the car window.

"It was the best, dad." Matthew answered for all of them. He and Ryan got in on one side of the car and Sara and Brad slid in on the other side.

"The movie was "Blue Hawaii" with Elvis Presley. It was so cool! Can we go to Hawaii some day?" Ryan was excited, sitting on the edge of the seat behind his dad.

"That's a good idea, Rye. Maybe your dad will spring for a trip to Hawaii for all of us. Now, that would be the coolest!" Mark loved planting these little seeds and watching them grow.

"Yeah, dad," Brad jumped in. "We could start planning it and saving up for it. How much would it cost?"

"A whole lot more than we have right now. It might take us a while to save up but it could be done if we plan it right." Paul was a great planner. He didn't want to discourage the kids. He liked them to have goals...realistic goals that they could eventually achieve. "Let's talk to mom about it."

"Yeah, let's talk to mom about it, daddy." Sara knew he loved it when she called him daddy."

"Sweetie, I think that's a real good idea. There's your mother, now."

They slowly pulled the car into the circle drive. Amy and Janie were sitting out by the fish pond visiting and enjoying a glass of ice tea in the perfect summer evening air.

"Hi, kids! How was the movie and the ice cream social?" Amy could see that the kids were excited. "There's a pitcher of ice tea and a pitcher of lemonade on the front porch for anyone who's interested, chocolate chip cookies, too." Amy and Janie made fresh ice tea and lemonade as they talked about their adventure earlier that evening.

"Mom, we all want to go to Hawaii together!" Sara announced, to the surprise of her mother and Amy. "They showed Blue Hawaii tonight with Elvis Presley. It was so beautiful there. We all want to go and we want to go together. Mr. Phillips said it might take us a while, but we can save up for it. Can we go? Can we, mom? It would be the greatest!"

"I would love to go to Hawaii! How about it, Amy?"

"Absolutely, Paul and I have talked about taking the kids on a real vacation. We get so busy with work and school that sometimes our vacation plans get pushed aside. Let's make this one a reality. Let's really plan it and do it!"

"Dad, did you hear that? Mom wants to go! We can save up for it. We can go to Hawaii just like in the Elvis movie!" Ryan was more than a little excited, as all the kids were, with thoughts of the sandy beaches, the warm blue ocean waters, and the surf of Waikiki.

The kids were all gathered around now, full of chatter about the movie and the ice cream social at the Fireman's Hall and how they could save for the trip to Hawaii.

Overhead, a blanket of twinkling stars filled the velvet night sky. The Milky Way seemed clearer than ever before. The stars always seemed brighter and more abundant at the lake.

"It's especially clear tonight. How about getting the telescope out, boys?" Paul knew they would all enjoy star-gazing together.

"I'll get it, dad." Ryan called, and ran past everyone into the house.

The chatter continued but was soon interrupted with a sudden loud bang that came from the boy's bedroom. Everyone jumped to their feet and ran toward the house.

"Ryan, are you all right? What happened? What was that noise?" Amy was first to reach the boy's bedroom.

Ryan was lying on the floor with telescope in hand. Grandpa's old fishing boat had fallen on top of him and he was pinned beneath it. Books, toys, and games that once rested on the fishing boat's old wooden shelves were strewn around him on the floor.

"Get this thing off of me. It's too heavy." Ryan was beginning to cry, not that he was physically hurt but more embarrassed than anything.

"Ryan, are you okay? Are you hurt?" Paul was kneeling down beside him now looking to see if he was bleeding. "Hold still while we lift the boat."

"Okay, dad," Ryan whimpered.

Paul and Mark lifted the old fishing boat just enough so that Ryan could wiggle out from underneath it.

"Are you bleeding anywhere?" Amy was right there beside him comforting him and stroking his hair. She was relieved to see that he wasn't hurt, just shaken a little.

Ryan sat on the floor for a minute rubbing his legs that were marked by the weight of the boat.

"I knew where the telescope was. Brad and I put it there the last time we used it. I stood on the bottom shelf of the boat to reach it but the shelf broke and the boat fell back on top of me." Ryan took a deep breath and stood up.

Brad, Sara, and Matthew were gathering the toys, books, and games from the floor and neatly stacking them on the bed.

"We're just glad you aren't hurt." Amy gave him a little pat on the behind.

"Mark, help me stand the boat upright so we can check out the broken shelf. I'm surprised it gave way. This thing is really built." Paul and Mark positioned themselves to lift the old boat. "Okay, on three: one, two, and three." Together they easily lifted the heavy old wooden boat up on end while everyone stood watching.

"Oh, my God," Amy shrieked in awe. "Look!"

All eyes focused on the bottom shelf of the upright boat. The shelf had broken away from the frame on one side and took a section of the old plank hull boards out with it. A dozen old shiny gold coins spilled out onto the floor from the opening.

"What's this?" Paul reached down and picked up a couple of the gold coins to examine them. "These are really *old*. Check this out." He flipped one to Mark.

The gold coins were smooth as silk and unlike anything that any of them had ever seen before.

"Where did these come from? We're going to have to take these coins to a professional in the city. Hopefully, they will have some history on them and some idea of their worth." Paul knelt down beside the broken shelf in the old boat to inspect the opening.

"I can't believe it! It's the treasure boat! It's the one that the townspeople have been talking about for years. The one with the hidden treasure! This *has* to be it!" Janie was certain. "Also, I hear that it's finder-keepers!"

"I wonder if your grandfather knew what was hidden in his old fishing boat." Amy posed the question to Paul.

"I don't know, but maybe that's why his grandpa passed it down to him and my dad made sure that we passed it down to you two boys. Maybe he *did* know." Paul was pleased but also puzzled.

"Wow! How much money do you think is in there? Maybe it's a lot? Maybe it's millions and millions of dollars?" Ryan had a great imagination. But they all were thinking the same thing.

"Well, let's take a look!" Paul reached in and pulled out an old dirty cloth sack with a large tear in the side. The leather tie strings were still wrapped tightly around the neck of the sack. The old sack was heavy. He needed two hands to pull it up and out from it's resting place. Behind it was another cloth sack, and then another, and another. A total of four sacks sat in a row on the floor in front of them. "That's it. There must be three our four hundred coins in each sack, maybe more. I have no idea of their worth, but we'll find out."

"We're rich! We're rich! Can I have a new bike and my own television?" Matthew was feeling a lot better now with the thought of all the goodies the gold could bring.

"Just hold on son. We don't even know if we can keep this." Amy hated to dampen his excitement but she needed to keep it real for everyone's sake.

"Mom, dad," Brad interrupted. "Now can we *all* go to Hawaii and we won't have to save up for it!"

For a moment there was silence as the thought sunk in. Then all the kids cheered with excitement.

"Brad, I definitely think that can be arranged." Paul looked at Mark and Janie standing arm-in-arm. "How about it, are you two game?"

"Oh, yeah! Definitely and without a doubt! I'll even get out the old grass skirt that I have hiding under the bed!" Mark bent his knees, waved his arms, and swayed his hips with his rendition of the hula. "I'll have to start practicing my moves, especially those 'round-the-world hip gyrations."

"Mark, you don't have a grass skirt, you nut!"

"Janie, baby doll, there are still things you don't know about me!" Mark winked and lifted his upper lip Elvis style…but he didn't miss a single sway.

Everyone laughed and joined in dancing the hula with him.

It was the perfect ending to the perfect day and another memory of fun and adventure at the lake.

The End

"Rhythm is something you either have or don't have,
but when you have it, you have it all over."

Elvis Presley

ELVIS AARON PRESLEY
1935 - 1977

ঙ্গ

Elvis Aaron Presley was born to Vernon and Gladys Presley in a two-room house in Tupelo, Mississippi on January 8, 1935. His twin brother, Jessie Garon, was stillborn, leaving Elvis to grow up as an only child. He and his parents moved to Memphis, Tennessee in 1948. Elvis graduated from Humes High School there in 1953.

Elvis was influenced by the pop and country music of the time, the gospel music he heard in church, at the all-night gospel sings he frequently attended, and the black R&B he absorbed on historic Beale Street as a Memphis teenager.

In 1954, Elvis began his singing career with the legendary Sun Records label in Memphis. In late 1955, his recording contract was sold to RCA Victor. By 1956, he was an international sensation. With a sound and style that uniquely combined his diverse musical influences and challenged the social and racial barriers of the time, he ushered in a whole new era of American music and popular culture.

Elvis starred in 33 successful films, made history with his television appearances and specials, and received great acclaim through his many, often record-breaking, live concert performances on tour and in Las Vegas.

Globally, Elvis sold over one billion records, more than any other artist. His American sales earned him gold, platinum or multi-platinum awards for 131 different albums and singles, far more than any other artist.

Among his many awards and accolades Elvis received 14 Grammy nominations (3 wins) from the National Academy of Recording Arts & Sciences, the Grammy Lifetime Achievement Award, which he received at age 36, and was named one of the Ten Outstanding Young Men of the Nation for 1970 by the United States Jaycees.

Without any of the special privileges his celebrity status might have afforded him, Elvis honorably served his country in the U.S. Army.

His talent, good looks, sensuality, charisma, and good humor endeared him to millions, as did the humility and human kindness he demonstrated throughout his life.

Known the world over by his first name, he is regarded as one of the most important figures of twentieth century popular culture.

Elvis died at his Memphis home, Graceland, on August 16, 1977...but did he really.

"Until we meet again,
may God bless you as he has blessed me."

Elvis Presley

CPSIA information can be obtained
at www.ICGtesting.com
Printed in the USA
FFOW04n1350040116
20105FF